The

Vision

Jessica Sorensen

For information:
http://jessicasorensensblog.blogspot.com/

Cover Photograph by Shutterstock
Cover Design by Mae I Design and Photography
www.maeidesign.com

The Vision — Book 3
ISBN 978-1466415157

Chapter 1

I kept having these dreams, or maybe they were more like nightmares. In them, Alex and I are standing out by the entrance to The Underworld. The lake is frozen and the trees are iced over with icicles dripping from the branches. The sky is as dark as a shadow and the air chills me to the bone. Alex's arms are wrapped tightly around me. We stay at the edge of the frozen water, clutching onto one another as if our lives depend on it.

The wind is blowing my hair into my face. There is a hollowness to the outside, like nothing is there but Alex and I, as if the whole world is empty. As we hold each other, a thought occurs to me that we are not supposed to be together, and if we don't let go, we will die. I look up at Alex and tell him my thoughts, but he always shushes me as he brushes my hair away from my face

"It will be alright," he whispers, but his bright green eyes tell me the opposite. *It won't be okay*, they say.

I open my mouth to tell him that I know he's lying, but a crackle ripples through the air and sucks the words away from my lips. I see them—the black hooded figures emerging from the trees, like an army of ice-monsters heading to destroy us.

I look at Alex, wanting him to say something—to do something—but he never does. He just sweeps my hair back and pulls me closer to him.

"It will be alright," he whispers one last time, and then I am suffocated by light. I hold onto Alex and take a deep breath as I am engulfed by warmth.

It will be alright.

But will it? Because every time I have this dream, I always wake up, lying on the floor of the cabin, stuck out in the middle of the snow-buried mountains. And in the snow lies my weakness. *Praesidium.* The one thing that renders me of my Foreseer power and binds me to the cabin for as long as Stephan wishes. Yes, I always wake up from my dream, but sometimes I wish I wouldn't.

Chapter 2

The bathroom faucet had the most annoying drip. Drip...drip...drip...over and over and over again. It was driving me crazy.

I'd been stuck in the cabin, where Stephan had left me, for nine days. And each morning I watched the sun rise through the barred window, was another morning where my sanity was coming to its end. If I thought my life with Marco and Sophia had been lonely, then I had no idea what lonely was, because this was the mere definition of lonely.

There was nothing in the cabin besides a bathroom. Stephan had left a box of food, I guess, not wanting me to starve to death. He wanted me alive—he made that very clear. He just wanted my mind and emotions gone, which, if things kept going the way they were, would probably happen pretty quickly.

I wasn't in that great a shape either. The spot where I hit my head on the rock, when Nicholas had shoved me down, constantly hurt, and I worried it might be getting infected. There was also only one blanket in the cabin and I constantly had to keep it wrapped around me, otherwise, I would freeze to death.

It was the same thing every day for nine days straight. I sat on the cold, hardwood floor, curled up in a blanket that smelled like dust and moth balls, and stared out at the snowy mountains that were decorated with marble-sized, lavender balls of *Praesidium*.

But on the ninth day I lost it.

I was lying on the floor tracing the cracks in the floorboards with my fingers, when I suddenly realized something. Before I knew what I was doing, I stood up and went over to the front door. I swung it open and, ignoring the blast of Arctic wind that smacked me in the face, I stepped out into the snow, barefoot and in shorts, with a blanket wrapped around my shoulders.

I wasn't sure where I was going, or if I would even make it very far, but I knew I could not stay here and give up.

Stephan would not win. Either I would escape, or I would die trying.

I would not let the world end.

I started down the mountain, shivering, shaking, and chattering until my muscles felt like they were going to break. But I forced myself to keep going, keeping my eyes on the *Praesidium* as I walked, wishing desperately that the trail of lavender marbles would finally end so I could foresee my way back to Maryland.

But as the wind kicked up, and the air dipped even colder, I knew.

I was going to die.

There have been a few times in my life where I thought I was dead, but this was different. I had to be dead this time because all I could see was light—everywhere. Warm light. I had been in a light vision before, and Nicholas had informed me that these kinds of visions meant my future was dead. So that meant I was dead right now, right? Because all I could see was light.

"Gemma," a voice whispered. *"Can you hear me?"*

My body tensed. "Who is that?" I called out through the light.

"Come toward me," the voice echoed.

I blinked, searching the light for someone, but I couldn't tell what was up or down, or if I was even standing or sitting.

"I can't see you," I said. "The light's too bright."

"Yes, you can," the voice assured me. "You just have to look harder."

If the voice didn't sound so unfamiliar, then I would have thought I was talking to Nicholas, because it seemed like something he would say. But this voice was much deeper and belonged to someone older.

So, not wanting to be difficult to a stranger, I blinked a few times, trying to "look harder." Strangely enough, the light began to dim. Slowly at first, and then much quicker, until there was nothing left but a faint glow.

I was lying on a midnight-blue marble floor, staring up at what looked like a cathedral ceiling. I got to my feet and examined myself over. My skin was its normal pale color and it appeared that the cold hadn't frostbitten any of my toes or fingers.

"Hello!" I called out, turning in a slow circle. The pale light fogged my surroundings, making it hard for me to see. But I could vaguely make out a row of columns on each side of me and a statue not too far off in front. I walked toward the statue, taking each step carefully, afraid that at any second someone—or something—was going to jump out from behind one of the columns.

I managed to make it to the statue unharmed, and without anyone jumping out at me. It was a statue of a man carved out of white marble. There was something about the man's face that looked familiar, but what had me puzzled even more was that in his hands was a crystal ball.

"What in the world?" I mumbled to myself. I leaned in to get a closer look at the plaque mounted at the statue's feet. My pulse quickened as I read the plaque: Julian Lucas. Lucas? No. There was no way…Could this be a statue of my father?

I covered my mouth with my hands and started to back away.

"Don't worry, it's just a statue."

I whirled around and then jumped back when I came face-to-face with a man that had a striking resemblance to the statue, only he was alive and breathing.

"Oh my God." My voice trembled. I couldn't believe it. His eyes…the color…violet. "Dad?"

He smiled. "Hello, Gemma."

Chapter 3

I had thought the alarming violet color of my eyes had been created from the star's energy. But I was wrong because the man standing before me had the exact same alarming shade of violet radiating from his eyes.

"I—I...can't..." Apparently, I had forgotten how to speak.

He gave me an understanding smile. "I know, it's shocking, isn't it?"

My eyes were wide as I nodded. "Yeah...it is."

We stared at each other, not believing what we were seeing. He looked so much like me; the same color of brown hair, the same pale skin—only his was creased with wrinkles—and of course the same shade of violet in his eyes.

"Am I dead?" I finally asked.

He shook his head. "Not quite."

"Not quite?" I asked, trying not to panic. "Does that mean I'm going to be, then?"

He considered this carefully. "While you were walking down the mountain, you passed out and took yourself here in vision form."

I swallowed hard. "So my body is still back on the mountain freezing to death?"

"Yes, but don't worry, today isn't the day you're going to die, Gemma." He turned around, the strange silver robe he was wearing swishing behind him. He motioned for me to follow him. "We only have a few minutes before you have to go back, and I have something very important I need to show you."

"Okay..." I followed him, glancing around as I walked, wondering what this place was. "What do you need to show me?"

He looked at me, his violet eyes sparkling in the pale-yellow light that fluttered through the room. "I'm going to show you how you're going to save the world."

I don't know why, but I just about laughed at him. "You're going to show me," I pointed at myself, "how *I'm* going to save the world?"

"You sound like you don't believe it's possible," he said

I shrugged. "It's just that I've seen things that have led me to believe otherwise."

"You have seen them in your visions," he said, not as a question, but as a statement.

I gaped at him. "So, you know about my visions?"

He gave me a small smile as he turned down a hall-way, lined with more columns and a ceiling swirled with yellows and blues that reminded me of Vincent van

Gogh's *The Starry Night.* "Where do you think you got the gift?"

"So you're a Foreseer." I wasn't really surprised by this, seeing how I had been told multiple times that abilities, such as the Foreseer ability, were usually inherited. Plus, I just saw the statue of him holding a crystal ball.

He nodded. "I am. And, like you, I also have unique abilities."

Now that shocked me and I tripped over my own feet, but caught myself before I dove onto the marble floor. "The same abilities as me?" I asked

"Yes, but that is a story for another time," he told me, looking sad. "Right now, you need to save the world."

I had a ton of questions. I mean, this was my first time meeting him, and I wanted to know about him. But there was an urgency in his voice that kept me quiet.

At the end of the hall, a stairway stretched up to a mausoleum-like building. Two massive columns formed an entryway around the door, and at the top of the door, a bright red light glowed from the screen-covered window.

"What is this place?" I asked, hoping that it just *looked* like a mausoleum.

He didn't answer as he walked up the stairs to the mausoleum in question. I followed him, the marble steps feeling cold underneath my bare feet as I climbed up the stairs. I was nervous and my heart fluttered in my chest as my father opened the door. The hinges creaked loudly, as if it had been sealed shut for ages. Then he stepped in, and, with great hesitance, I did too.

It was dark inside the tiny room and the air was damp. The ceiling dripped with muddy water and the once white-tiled floor was stained brown with age. There were no windows and the column walls were cracked and worn away. Red lanterns softly lit a trail of red light down a narrow hallway.

"This way," my father told me, gesturing down the hall.

The air grew heavier with each step I took. Columns continued to line the walls and I noticed that each one had an eye carved on it. Each eye was a different shape and color, and in the pupil was a circle that wrapped an S—the Foreseers' mark. I wondered if this place was some kind of place for Foreseers.

"What is this place?" I asked.

My father shook his head. "A place where no one wants to be."

His words scared me, but before I could press him further, we reached the end of the hall where a large blue trunk, trimmed with gold, sat on top of an antique table. My father raised the lid slowly, and I held my breath as he reached inside the trunk and took out a crystal ball.

He held the crystal ball out to me, his eyes gleaming a bright violet in the light it casted. "This, Gemma, is how you're going to save the world."

I eyed the crystal ball warily. "With a crystal ball?"

13

He took my hand, his skin ice-cold, and set the crystal ball in it. "With this and your power."

It wasn't like any of the other crystal balls I had seen. It radiated a glittery, purple glow that came from a star-shaped light in the center. It was beautiful, that was for sure, and in a strange way, the purple glow kind of reminded me of my eyes.

I shook my head. "I don't understand. How is my power going to save the world? I thought my power was what ended it?" I raised the crystal ball. "And what is *this* for?"

"I'm talking about your Foreseer power, not the stars'," he said, shutting the lid of the trunk. He stood there silently for a moment, looking as though he was struggling to tell me something important. "I have done things in my life that have led me to this place. Things that are unforgivable—things which you will understand soon." He paused. "Gemma, I need you to put the future back."

"Okay…how do I do that exactly?" I glanced down at the crystal ball sparkling in my hand. "And how do I use this?"

"That, I cannot tell you."

"Why not?"

"Because you have to figure it out on your own." He smiled softly. "You and I are unique cases, even for our unique kind. We can both travel into visions without the assistance of a crystal, so, with enough strength, you

14

should be able to change the vision I erased and recreated."

I stared at him, confused. "I'm sorry, but I don't understand. You *changed* a vision?"

He looked at me with regret in his eyes. "The vision I changed was so the world would end."

I was taken back and I almost dropped the crystal ball. "You made it so the world would end? How...why?"

"That's not important," he said, his voice growing sharp. "What's important is that you fix it—change it back to how it's supposed to be. You need to make sure the world doesn't end up like it did in the vision you saw."

I shivered as I remembered. "The one where everything ends in ice—the one where Stephan wins?"

A look of darkness passed across his face when I mentioned Stephan's name. "Yes, that's what you need to stop from happening."

I stood there, hardly believing what I was hearing. The first time I ever meet my father, and he informs me that he changed a vision so Stephan would be able to end the world in ice.

"So how do I change the world's future back to what it is supposed to be?" I asked, turning the crystal ball in my hand.

He tapped the crystal ball with his finger. "Everything you need to know is in here." He touched his finger to the side of my head. "And in here."

15

Okay, this was making no sense. "How do I use it then?" I stared perplexedly at the crystal ball. "Just like a regular crystal ball?"

He turned his back to me and started down the hall. "It's time for you to return...you're not even supposed to be here. Good-bye, Gemma. I have great confidence that you'll be able to fix my mistakes."

I started after him, desperate to know more, but strangely, the walls seemed to be blurring away. It was like I was having trouble seeing—and walking.

My father kept moving further and further away from me as the hall flickered in and out of focus. I tried to chase after him, but it felt like I was only putting more distance between us. "But I don't understand any of it! How am I supposed to change visions? And how do I know which ones to change?" I stopped, my feet feeling too heavy to move. "Dad, I don't understand!"

"Don't worry," he called over his shoulder. "You will."

Before I could say anything else, the walls closed in, and everything went black.

Chapter 4

Water splashed across my face, soaking my skin and drenching my clothes. My body felt like it had been run over by a truck and my eyelids were as heavy as lead. I could hear the ocean lulling, but it didn't make sense since I was up in the mountains.

Water hit me in the face again, and I opened my eyes right as a wave crashed over me. I scrambled to my feet, hacking up water as I scurried out of the ocean's reach. I couldn't believe what I was seeing. I was standing on a sandy shore, the dark-blue ocean extending out before me, the golden sun reflecting against the water. Behind me, houses lined the beach, and one house in particular—a light-blue one—I knew would be the house where I would find my mom, Alex, Aislin, and Laylen.

Clutching the crystal ball my dad gave me, I ran for the house, the sand burning against the soles of my feet. People dotted the beach, and they probably thought I was crazy; soaked from head-to-toe, holding a crystal ball as I sprinted like mad. I didn't care, though. They could stare. I was no longer on the mountain and that was all that mattered at the moment.

I made it to the house panting and charged up the wooden steps of the back porch. "Mom," I called out, throwing open the back door. "Mom!"

I moved across the kitchen and went into the living room. No one was there and the only noise was the tick-tock of the wall clock.

Where were they? Did they go looking for me? Probably. I had, after all, been missing for nine days. Great. I needed to find a phone and see if I could get a hold of someone; let them know I was back.

I have no idea why people thought it was a good idea to get rid of house phones. Yes, there are cell phones, but cell phones don't do any good when you don't own one.

I searched the house, looking for a phone, but ten minutes later, I was still phoneless. I was just about to walk out the front door to go find someone who would let me use their phone, when the door opened on its own and Alex entered. His dark-brown hair was messy and not in an intentional way like it usually was. The color of his green eyes popped against the black t-shirt he was wearing. My happiness and thrill of seeing him bubbled up inside me and I just about ran over and threw my arms around him. It was a bit of a shock, feeling this way toward him, and I wondered how deep my feelings for him were getting. It was extremely confusing to think about.

But I resisted the urge to run over to him, remembering Stephan's words: *If you stay close to each other for too long the star's power will fade out. And so will you and Alex.*

"Hey, did you find him?" Alex asked, before I got a chance to speak. He shut the door and walked up to me, creating a bit of a problem because the electricity was firing up like a firework show.

I took a step back. "Did I find who?"

He furrowed his eyebrows. "Laylen."

I was so confused. "Why? Did something happen to him?"

Alex looked as confused as I felt. "Yeah, he disappeared, remember? Everyone is out looking for him. I take it, though, you didn't find him."

WTF. What was he talking about? "But I've been gone for nine days."

He looked at me like I was insane. "No, you haven't."

"Yes, I have…oh…" My mouth fell open as it dawned on me.

"Gemma, what's wrong?" His bright-green-eyed gaze moved all over me. "Why are your clothes all wet?" He took the crystal ball from me and turned it over in his hand. "Where did you get this?"

I didn't answer. I just stood there, with my mouth agape, struggling to grasp what was going on. My father had sent me back to before Nicholas had captured me and handed me over to Stephan—before I had spent nine days locked away in the cabin. And he did not send me back in

19

vision form. I was here in the present, and I could communicate and touch things...I think.

Without even thinking, I reached out and placed my hand on Alex's arm. The electricity surged with our contact.

"Holy crap," I whispered. I took the crystal ball from him and sank down on the couch that smelled of salt water and sand. "I can't believe it."

Alex sat down beside me, a concerned look on his face. "Gemma, please tell me what's wrong."

I swallowed hard. "Something happened to me."

"Okay...do you want to tell me what it is?"

I slowly nodded and then started to explain everything that had happened to me—or didn't happen, I guess I should say, because if I was here at this very moment, then those nine days at the cabin never took place. I was back where I started, only now I had a unique crystal ball in my hand and a ton of new unanswered questions.

I knew right away that I shocked the heck out of Alex. His eyes were wide and his mouth was slightly hanging open. It took him a minute, after I finished explaining, to say something

"So what you're saying," he said slowly, "is that right now we're nine days in the past."

I shook my head. "I don't think so. I think the nine days I spent at the cabin were somehow erased." I set the crystal ball in my lap, thinking about how my father said he erased a vision and recreated it. "I think, somehow, my father erased and recreated some of the events of my life, so that I would end up back here."

"So that my father never got a hold of you?" Alex asked, still looking really lost.

It was weird having him ask me questions, and it kind of sucked because I didn't have answers to give him. "I don't know...I'm not sure how it works. He only told me he erased a vision and recreated it to change the outcome of the world's future." I twisted the crystal ball in my hand, staring at the glowing purple star inside. "He said he changed it so that the world would end the way I saw it in my ice vision."

Alex's forehead creased over. "Are you saying that he made it so my father could end the world?"

I felt kind of ashamed of my father. "I think so."

Alex stared off into space, thinking about what I said. "So where was your father exactly?"

"I have no idea. He never told me. He wouldn't tell me anything, really, just that I was going to save the world." I held up the crystal ball. "And that everything I needed to know was inside this....Oh yeah, and in my head."

Alex dragged his fingers through his hair, tugging at the roots. "But none of what you said makes sense. Foreseers aren't supposed to be able to control how the future turns out—they're not supposed to recreate visions to their liking."

21

"Yeah...but I don't know...it seems like it could be possible. I mean, look at me. I can travel around wherever I want by using my Foreseer ability, without the aid of a crystal ball."

"Yeah, but you are..." He trailed off as I gave him a cold stare. He was about to say different, and I really disliked being called that. "Unique," he finished, with a teasing smile that focused all of my attention on his lips, which painfully reminded me that I was never going to be able to kiss those lips again unless I figured out a way to get rid of the star's power.

His face fell. "What's wrong?"

I shook my head, not sure how explain that we were not supposed to be together; that the Blood Promise we made, to be together forever, was useless; that if we stayed close to one another for too long, there was a possibility we could kill each other. Of course, this was all based on if Stephan had told the truth.

"I have to—" I started

The front door flew open and smacked against the wall, rattling the shelves on it. Aislin burst in, her cheeks pinked with heat, her golden-brown hair a mess and her clothes covered in dirt and sand.

"What's wrong?" Alex quickly stood up from the couch

Aislin shook her head, tears streaking her cheeks. "Laylen...Lay..." She burst into hysterical sobs.

I jumped to my feet. "What about Laylen? Did something happen to him?" I asked, in a panic-stricken voice as the reality that saving the world wasn't my only responsibility. I also had to save a vampire who was dealing with blood thirst issues. Blood thirst issues that I caused by begging him to bite me so he wouldn't die.

Aislin sobbed hard. "I can't—I can't."

"Just spit it out," Alex said unsympathetically.

Looking hurt, Aislin wiped her tears away and pulled herself together. "I can't find him anywhere."

"Okay," Alex said in an unfeeling tone. "Well, freaking out isn't going to help us find him."

Aislin fixed him with an angry glare. "You don't need to be rude. I'm just a little upset, okay?" She looked like she might start crying again. "I never got to tell him I was," she sniffed back her tears, "sorry...for everything." She burst into sobs and ran off to her room.

"You know, sometimes I'm grateful I can shut off my emotions." Alex turned to me. "It keeps me from doing things like that."

I stared at him, half agreeing and half disagreeing. "Not all emotions are bad," I said.

His bright green eyes burned with intensity. "Aren't they?" His voice wobbled and he was breathing loud. He reached for me, about to touch me, and for a moment I just stood there, wanting him to touch me. But then I remembered we couldn't get close—not until we knew for sure that it wouldn't kill us.

23

I backed away from him.

His expression slipped into confusion as he pulled his hand back. "What's wrong?"

"We can't..." I took a deep breath, gesturing my hand back and forth between us. "You and I can't—"

"Your head's bleeding," he cut me off, staring at my head.

"Huh?"

He pointed at the side of my head. "There's blood all over the side of your head."

I touched my head and a warm, sticky substance coated my fingers. I pulled my hand away—blood. I went over to an oval mirror hanging on the wall and examined my head. On the left side, a cut ran across my scalp. And it had to be a fresh cut because blood was still oozing out of it and dripping down my hair.

"What happened?" Alex moved up behind me, inspecting the cut on my head. "You weren't bleeding before, were you? I didn't notice if you were."

"No, I don't think so." My eyes were fixed on the cut. Why was it so familiar? Not just the cut, but the pain that was starting to spread through my skull—a blinding pain like I had smacked my head on a rock or something...my eyes widened. "Oh my God."

"What is it?" Alex asked, alarmed.

"I think..." I set the crystal ball down on the desk and bolted for the back door.

Alex chased after me. "Where are you going?"

"I think something's wrong," I answered, leaping down the back porch steps. I took off across the beach, heading for the cliff area where Nicholas had once knocked me out, before taking me to the cabin. I needed to see if there was blood on the rock I hit my head on. If there was blood on it then that meant...Well, I had no idea what it meant, just that it meant something wasn't right.

"Gemma!' Alex yelled from right behind me. "Where the heck are you going?"

I pointed at the rocky cliffs, pushing past a few people that were standing in my way. "There...I have to see something." I slowed to a stop as I reached the cliffs.

Alex stopped beside me, panting. "What do you need to see?"

"I need to see if there's blood on the rock that Nicholas shoved me down on," I told him, heading down the path that twisted through the center of the cliffs.

"But I thought you said that didn't happen." Alex followed at my heels as we made our way further down the path. "That your father erased it?"

I glanced over my shoulder at him. "I thought he did but now..." I shook my head. "I have no idea what's going on, but if there's blood on one of these rocks back in here, then something's up—something's not right." My head was pounding and blood was trickling down my ear. I pressed my hand against the wound and picked up my pace, ignoring the rocks cutting my bare feet.

When I finally reached the end of the path, I swear my heart just about stopped. And all my confusion multiplied.

"What the?" Alex moved to the side of me and squinted at the ground. "What is that?"

"It's....me?" I said, staring down at myself, lying on the ground, in a pool of blood. "Am I in a vision?" I wondered out loud.

From my peripheral, I saw a dark figure appear, and I jumped back, knocking my shoulder into Alex's chest. Nicholas, who was usually annoyingly calm—well, unless he was being chased by a Water Faerie in The Underworld—looked about as shocked as I was.

His golden eyes widened as he glanced down at the "me" lying in the sand and then back at the real me.

"What on earth..." He trailed off and something abruptly clicked across his face. He knew exactly what was going on.

"Wow, Gemma," he said with genuine astonishment. "I am *very* impressed." He paused and then he lunged for me.

I don't have the reflexes of a cat at all, and Nicholas was skilled in the art of lunging. Luckily, for my sake, Alex's reflexes were that of a Keeper and with one swing of his fist, he knocked Nicholas out cold.

Nicholas' body slumped heavily to the ground.

Alex shook out his hand. "His head is as hard as a rock."

I would have laughed, except I was too occupied with the fact that there was another "me" lying on the ground. I stepped over Nicholas and gradually made my way over to her—or me. Was she real? Or was she just a vision? Hesitantly, I reached down and placed a hand gently on her arm. It was like I had stuck my fingers in an electrical outlet. My eyes zipped wide as a blaze of electricity—more powerful than anything I had ever felt—zipped through me. I gasped, feeling the moment erase, as if it had never existed. The unconscious "me" buzzed with static, like bad reception on TV, finally blinking and fading out into nothing.

My hand fell down onto the warm sand, and I stared at the empty spot in utter shock.

"Gemma." Alex placed a hand on my shoulder. "What the hell just happened?"

His hand fell from my shoulder as I stood to my feet. My mind was so wired with electricity I thought my head was going to explode.

"I think I need to lie down." I staggered sideways and then collapsed to the ground.

Chapter 5

Light…everywhere, surrounding me, blinding me. Alex and I by the lake, holding onto one another. *It will be okay.* Ice. So cold. Death. Shadows everywhere…suffocating me…I was dying…

My eyes shot open as I gasped for air. I clutched the bottom of my neck, hyperventilating as I bolted upright.

"Breathe." Alex patted me on the back. "Just breathe."

"I'm trying," I coughed. I took a few slow, deep breaths until my breathing returned to normal, and then I tried to get to my feet. But the world twirled and swayed and I sank back into the sand.

"What happened?" Alex asked, kneeling down in front of me, his eyes scanning me over for any visible evidence that I might be broken.

"It felt like I couldn't breathe," I told him.

Alex, being Alex, straightforwardly said, "That's because you stopped breathing."

"Oh," was all I could think of to say.

He touched the cut on my head and my scalp tingled with sparks. "Well, whatever just happened, it made the cut on your head seal itself up."

I lightly grazed the side of my head with the tips of my finger. "It doesn't hurt anymore either." I dropped my hand and gave him a puzzled look. "What do *you* think just happened?"

"I have no idea." He nodded his head at something behind me. "I wonder if he does, though."

I turned and found Nicholas still sprawled out in the sand, unconscious. "It looked like he might know something," I said, turning back to Alex. "But even if he did, what are the odds of him actually telling us?"

His bright green eyes sparkled deviously. "Oh, there are ways to get him to tell us." He got to his feet and dusted the sand off his jeans. "They're just not nice ways."

I kind of felt bad for Nicholas, which I know sounds very weird, considering everything he had done. But, I mean, he had no control over what he was—the Mark of Malefiscus did. Well, okay, I had to retract that statement because not every annoying and wrong thing Nicholas did was because of the mark. He was just as annoying before he was branded by the mark. But that didn't mean he deserved to be hurt.

I shielded my eyes from the sun's brightness as I stared up at Alex. "What are you going to do to him?"

He walked over to Nicholas. "We're going to go back and get Aislin, so she can transport him into the house." He paused, mulling something over. "I would drag him there myself, but I think it might look a little suspicious to some people."

29

Some people? Try all people. "Well, maybe I should just go get Aislin, in case he wakes up and tries to leave."

Alex's eyebrow curved up. "Can you even walk right now?"

Even though I was extremely dizzy, I was determined to show him I could. I gained control of my balance, before pushing myself to my feet. I rocked from side to side, and stumbled over to the wall of the cliff, bracing my hands against it.

"Gemma," Alex started to say, his tone full of worry.

"Just give me a second." *Alright, Gemma, one foot in front of the other…*Yeah, okay, that wasn't happening.

I collapsed to the ground, barely able to keep my eyes in focus. "Alright, you go get Aislin, and I'll stay here."

"Are you crazy?" Alex said.

"I'll be fine." I shooed him away with my hand. "Now hurry up and go get her."

"You won't be fine." He frowned at me. "And if he does wake up, he'll just take you."

He had a point, but...

"At least take the crystal ball he uses to travel with." I rested my heavy head against the cliff. "That way if he does wake up, he won't get very far."

"Do you know where he keeps it?"

"I think he keeps it in the pocket of his pants."

Alex gave me a blank stare. ""You want me to reach into the pocket of another guy's pants."

Oh my word. Guys were such babies sometimes.

Still not feeling up to standing, I crawled over to Nicholas, reached in his pocket, and took out his ruby-filled traveling crystal ball that shimmered red when it caught in the light of the sun.

Alex took the crystal ball from me and chucked it over the cliff. "Alright, let's go."

I gave a slow nod, not wanting to stand up and walk. Every part of my body was weak, like all the energy had been sucked out of me.

Alex held his hand out and helped me to my feet. I felt like I was standing on an out-of-control merry-go-round.

I clutched onto his arm. "I think something's wrong with me."

"You're just figuring that out?" he teased, but there was concern in his tone.

"Ha ha," I said sarcastically.

He laughed.

I saw spots and my ears popped. "I think...there's something..." I trailed off as I fell toward the ground.

Alex caught me. "Careful," he said, steadying me. Then he lifted me up into his arms.

The electricity flowing from him was like a peaceful lullaby, singing me to sleep. But even through my dazed-out brain, I knew it was wrong. Alex was not supposed to be carrying me.

"You can't...be...near...me," I murmured, drifting in and out of consciousness.

He shushed me, and I was overcome by sleepiness. I rested my head against his chest and a second later, I was out.

I woke up lying in a bed in a room with sky-blue walls. My vision was back to normal and my head was much clearer. I gradually sat up, just in case I was hit with another spout of dizziness. But my equilibrium seemed to be fixed. Thank God. I actually thought I was broken; that whatever took place back on the beach had permanently blinded me or something.

The door cracked open and Alex peered in. He looked shocked to see me awake.

"Feeling better?" he asked, pushing the door open the rest of the way.

I stretched my arms out above my head and yawned. "Yeah."

He sat down on the bed and nervous energy was radiating off him. "You freaked the heck out of me back there, you know that?"

"Sorry," I said. "I don't know what happened...it was like all my energy was sucked away from me or something."

He was looking at me in a way that made my skin glow with heat. He placed a hand on my cheek. "You *really* freaked me out."

My heart pounded inside my chest. Why was he looking at me like that? It was making me feel like I was suffocating.

I flinched away from him.

He frowned, his hand still hovering in the air. "What's wrong?"

Not looking at him, I took a deep breath. "I need to tell you something."

He tucked a strand of my hair behind my ear. "Okay, what is it?"

I shivered from his touch. I wished he would have acted like this when I first met him. "It's about you and me," I said, meeting his eyes.

He pressed his lips together, looking amused. "Oh, yeah?"

He still had his fingers in my hair and it took all my energy not to lean my head into his hand and shut my eyes. "Your father told me something about you and me when I was up at the cabin," I told him, my voice trembling.

He looked worried. "Was it something bad?"

I nodded. "It is."

"But you were never up at the cabin, so that means it doesn't matter, right?"

I choked back the strangling feeling rising up inside me, knowing that once I said it out loud, it would become very real. "I know, but I'm sure it still applies." I paused. "He told me that if you and I were close to each other for too long then the star's power would eventually fade away and you and I would fade along with it."

I held my breath, waiting for him to get riled up, but all he did was sit there, staring at me. I was just starting to wonder if I had shocked the words right out of him, when he shut down. The scary part was that I swear I actually could see it; the emotion slipping out of his eyes and leaving nothing in its place.

"Well, okay then." He stood up and headed for the door.

"That's all you have to say?" I sprung to my feet, kind of pissed off that he wasn't as upset as I was.

"What do you want me to say?" he asked with an uncaring shrug. "We can't be near each other, so we won't."

I glared at him. "Well, we could at least make sure it's true before we do."

He opened the door. "Why would we do that?"

I was filled with the urge to shove him. "Why are you being such a jerk?"

He let out a frustrated breath and turned to face me. "What do you want from me, Gemma? We can try to find out if there's some truth to it, but it's probably true—it's probably why he never wanted us to be near each other in the first place."

Whoa. I never thought of that, and I think, up until this point, I was grasping onto the hope that Stephan had been feeding me a lie.

"I…um…" I was at a loss for words.

We stared at one another, unsure of what to do or say, while the electricity danced around us, laughing at us, taunting us, torturing us with its existence.

Aislin appeared in the doorway. "He's awake."

I tore my eyes away from Alex. "Who is? Nicholas?"

She nodded and Alex pushed past her.

Aislin gave me a funny look, but I didn't feel like explaining what was going on.

"Is my mom back, yet?" I asked.

She had changed out of her dirty clothes and her hair was back to its normal perfect state. "No, I haven't heard from her since we all split up to go find Laylen," she said. "But maybe it's a good sign she's not back. Maybe she found him and is trying to get him to come back."

Maybe, but it worried me that she wasn't back yet. It just didn't seem like a great idea for my mom—who had just been freed from The Underworld a day ago—to be out by herself looking for a vampire with blood thirst issues.

"I know it's not the best situation," Aislin told me like she read my mind. "But I'm sure she's okay."

"I hope they're both okay," I said, but something in my gut told me this was not the case.

Chapter 6

"Is this really necessary?" I asked Alex for about the millionth time.

He shrugged and popped his knuckles. "Maybe."

He wasn't being rude or anything, he was just acting all "whatever." This was the attitude he had given me for the last half an hour as Aislin and I stood out in the hot, humid garage and watched Alex try to beat the information out of Nicholas.

Nicholas seemed to be finding Alex's beatings amusing. He kept laughing every time Alex punched him. I swear I was really starting to wonder if faeries were a little bit crazy.

Nicholas' hands were tied to a pipe that ran along the ceiling. His lip was bleeding, and the rope was cutting into his wrists, causing blood to drip down his arms and soak the green t-shirt he was wearing. Plus, I was pretty sure Alex had broken a couple of his ribs.

"Tell me what you know about what happened back there on the beach," Alex demanded. Like clockwork, Nicholas laughed at him and then Alex punched him in the stomach.

Nicholas laughed again, but I could see he was in a lot of pain by the way his expression twisted and his skin coated with sweat. "You know, it actually kind of tickles."

Alex clocked him in the stomach again, and I cringed at the cracking noise that had to be a rib breaking. "I could do this all day." Alex paced in front of him and then rammed his fist into Nicholas' side. Alex continued doing this over and over, his face reddening with anger the more Nicholas laughed.

"We should do something," I said to Aislin in a low voice.

She blinked at me helplessly. "Like what?"

"I don't know…" I pushed my shoulders back, trying to look confident as I marched over to Alex. "Stop it. I don't think he's going to tell you anything, even if he does know something."

Alex ignored me and raised his hand, preparing to swing.

I grabbed his arm, which I know was a very stupid thing to do for many different reasons. "Look, I know he's annoying and everything, but still…"

Alex was breathing erratically and the anger burning in his bright green eyes made me shrink back.

"Are you okay?" I asked in a calming voice.

He blinked a few times as if he was coming out of a raging state. Then he tore his arm away from me. "What are you doing? You can't touch me." So much anger burned from his eyes, and the sparks nipped madly at my skin.

"Is this really about getting information from Nicholas?" I whispered. "Or is it about what I told you?"

"Why would it be about that?" His voice cut through the air like a knife about to injure me. "It doesn't matter to me whether you and I can be together."

Okay, that stung. But I was pretty sure he was putting on a front—or at least I hoped he was. After learning about myself and about him, I knew that both of our emotions were a little bit...what would be a nice word for it...erratic. We don't show our true feelings sometimes, and I think it's because we're still learning how to.

"You don't mean that." My voice was barely a whisper

He opened his mouth, and then shut it again. Then he just looked at me with this confused, panicked expression. The electricity heated up. I heard Aislin say...something, but all I could focus on was his eyes and the buzzing and the—

Nicholas busted up laughing. "Oh my God, look at you two. You both want to be together so bad, yet, if you do, you'll kill each other. It's hilarious."

Alex and I blinked and then Alex was moving for Nicholas.

"What did you just say?" Alex growled, clenching his hands into fists.

Nicholas pressed back a smirk, his golden eyes twinkling wickedly. "I didn't say anything."

Alex took a few threatening steps toward him, the soles of his black DCs scuffing against the cement floor. "What do you know about Gemma and I killing one another?"

"What?" Aislin exclaimed, her loud voice echoing through the air. "What do you mean you'll kill each other?"

"We'll explain later." He waved her off, his gaze still glued on Nicholas. "Start talking."

Nicholas slowly shook his head and Alex raised his fist. With how much wrath was blazing in Alex's eyes, I worried that if he started swinging he might not stop this time.

Nicholas must have sensed it too. "Alright, alright...I'll tell you." He paused, contemplating something that I was sure was probably going to start trouble. "But I want something in return."

Alex was already shaking his head. "No way."

"Then no deal," Nicholas said while struggling to keep his footing.

"I don't think you're in much of a position to be making bargains," Alex said, raising a fist. "Or do I need to remind you of that?"

"What do you want?" I stepped in between them, if for nothing else, so I would no longer have to witness anymore punching.

39

"Gemma," Alex warned, but I held up my hand, my eyes on Nicholas. "What do you want?"

The humor erased itself from Nicholas' face. "I want to stay here."

My hand dropped, along with my jaw. "You want to what?"

"I want to stay here." Blood trickled down his wrists, and he winced as the rope swayed. "After I tell you what I know, I want to be able to hang around for a while."

Alex and I both shook our heads.

"No way." Alex's voice was unyielding.

"Yeah, I don't think that's such a good idea." I pointed to the Mark of Malefiscus on Nicholas' forearm. "Especially considering you have that."

"That's why I want to stay," Nicholas said. "If Stephan can't find me, then he can't make me do things for him."

I glanced at Alex. "Is that true?"

Alex shrugged. "I have no idea how the mark works."

I eyed Nicholas suspiciously. "How do we know you're telling the truth? I mean, I've seen what you were going to do to me back on the shore."

A grin spread across his face. "I bet you did. Tell me, did you just see it or did you actually live it?"

Why did the one person who seemed to have the answers have to be a very obnoxious faerie/Foreseer that loved to twist things around and make everything difficult?

I looked from Alex to Aislin. "What do you guys think we should do?"

"I don't know...do you think we can trust him?" Aislin asked Alex.

He took a deep breath and ran his fingers through his hair. "I don't know."

This was giving me a headache. I rubbed the sides of my temples, trying to make all the stress disappear. That's when I caught sight of the scar on the palm of my hand. I held my hand out if front of me and stared at the scar that marked my and Alex's Blood Promise to be together forever.

"I think I have an idea." I turned to Nicholas. "Would you be willing to *promise* that you wouldn't do anything harmful to anyone?"

Nicholas and Alex gave me a perplexed look. Then, realization spread across their faces.

"No way," Alex said, and at the same time Nicholas remarked, "Clever girl."

"Why not?" I asked Alex. "It's not like it's a bad thing or anything."

"Blood Promises can go wrong, Gemma." He frowned as he traced the scar on the palm of his hand. "The promise is unbreakable—you can't take it back. And if you say the wrong thing, you can end up making a promise you didn't intend to make."

"Is that what happened with us?" I asked, offended. "Did you say the wrong thing? Or is it that you just want to take it back?"

"No." He looked taken aback. "That's not what I meant. I was just saying things could go wrong...you could say the wrong thing and end up getting stuck with *him* forever."

Nicholas grinned as if this were a compliment.

I shook my head and let out a stressed sigh. "Okay, we'll have to be really careful then."

Alex leaned toward me and dropped his voice. "And even with the Blood Promise, if my father shows up, Nicholas more than likely will still have to do what he asks because I'm pretty sure the Mark of Malefiscus is more powerful than a Blood Promise."

"Then, I guess we will have to make sure your father doesn't find us." My voice trembled from Alex's closeness. *Focus*, I told myself. "If he might have some answers on how I can save the world, then I think it's worth the risk."

Alex still looked unconvinced, but I didn't care. I already made up my mind. I was going to do this. "Okay, you and I will make a Blood Promise. I'll promise you can stay here with us, and you'll promise that you'll answer all of my questions...truthfully. And, you won't harm any of us. Got it?"

He considered this. "I want one more thing."

I rolled my eyes. "What else do you want?"

He nodded his head at Aislin. "I want Witch Girl over there to try and find a way to get this thing off my arm."

I shot Aislin a questioning glance. "Can you do that?"

Aislin's green eyes went wide. "I don't know...I mean, there might be a spell that could remove a mark, but I've never heard of it, or I might not be powerful enough to actually pull it off."

"You know other witches, don't you?" Nicholas said in a rude tone. "Talk to them — see if they know how."

Aislin twisted her golden brown hair around her finger. "Maybe I could see if someone knows a spell that would do it."

"That's all I'm asking," Nicholas said.

"Alright, then." Aislin let go of her hair. "I'll see what I can do."

Nicholas' gaze landed on me. "So are you ready to do this?"

"Do you have a knife?" I asked Alex, holding my hand out.

"Why?" he asked, his arms crossed as he looked at me with irritation.

"So I can cut my hand and make the promise." I tapped my foot impatiently, waiting for him to hand over the knife I was almost certain he had.

He shook his head, frustrated. Then he reached into the pocket of his jeans and retrieved a silver pocket knife. "I still don't think this is a good idea." He reluctantly handed me the knife.

I flipped open the blade and winced at the sharp tip as it flashed in the florescent lighting of the garage. I tried to keep a steady hand as I held the knife up to the palm of my hand. "So, I just cut?"

Alex sighed and took the knife from me. "Give me your hand," he said and I did. He traced the scar on my palm with his finger, and then let my hand go. "Give me you other hand."

Confused, I gave him my other hand. "What? Can I not do the promise in the same place?"

He shook his head, his eyes locked on the palm of my hand. "No, you can. But that scar was from our promise."

It felt like a thousand butterflies were fluttering around in my stomach.

"Man, you two are going to kill each other quick, aren't you?" Nicholas remarked with a smirk.

Alex shot him a glare and then held the knife to my palm. "Okay, I'm going to cut your hand and his. Then you'll press your palms to his and repeat what I say, alright?"

I swallowed hard and nodded. "Alright."

"And be very careful that you repeat *exactly* what I say."

"Don't you need to untie him first?" I pointed over at Nicholas.

"I'm not going to let him go until the promise is made," Alex told me firmly. "You'll just have to reach up to his hand."

Well, it's a good thing I'm tall because it was going to be a really high reach to get Nicholas' hand; they were practically touching the ceiling.

Alex pressed the tip of the knife gently against the palm of my hand and then, very carefully, he made a small cut. Blood seeped out and my skin felt like it was on fire. Alex quickly went over to Nicholas, reached up to where his hands were bound, and with less carefulness, sliced the palm of Nicholas' hand. Blood oozed out of his skin and dripped down his arm.

Alex flipped the blade shut and tossed it on the cement floor. "Gemma, put your hand up to his."

I took a deep breath and, ignoring the flowery smell that always flowed off Nicholas, stood on my tiptoes and pressed my bleeding palm against Nicholas'. His closeness made me uncomfortable, along with the deviousness playing at his lips.

"We should have done this a long time ago." His breath was hot on my cheeks.

Glaring, I leaned my face away from him.

"Repeat *exactly* what I say," Alex said, holding my gaze. "*EGO votum permissum.*"

I spoke slowly so I wouldn't mess anything up. "*EGO... votum...permissum.*"

Alex swallowed hard. "*Vos subsisto hic quod Andron.*"

"*Vos...subsisto...hic quod...Andron.*" My voice shook.

"*Mos capto aufero vestri vestigium.*"

"*Mos capto...aufero...vestri...vestigium.*"

45

Alex and I both let out a breath of relief, and then Alex pointed a finger sharply at Nicholas. "You better repeat exactly what I say. No changing or adding anything, understand?"

Nicholas nodded, but there was a mischievous look in his eye that made me uneasy. "I understand."

Alex told him what to say, speaking his words vigilantly. Nicholas repeated what Alex said, and as far as I could tell he said each word correctly. But I had no idea what was being said, since I don't speak Latin, so I was putting a lot of trust in Alex. Strangely, I think I might have reached the point where I could do this.

After the Blood Promise was made, Alex cut the rope and freed Nicholas. Nicholas rubbed his bleeding wrist and wiped the blood from his lip with the bottom of his green t-shirt.

"Okay, tell us everything you know," Alex said, swiping the pocket knife off the floor.

"Can we at least sit down?" Nicholas asked with pain in his voice.

Alex shook his head and wiped the blade of the knife on his jeans, cleaning off the blood. "Tell us now."

Again, I kind of felt sorry for faerie boy. I mean, he looked like crap, and it wasn't going to do any harm to go sit down.

"We can go into the living room and sit," I told Nicholas. "If you want to?"

Alex shot me a dirty look.

I shrugged. "He's hurt."

Still glowering at me, Alex leaned over and whispered in my ear, "Feeling sorry for him is only going to get you into trouble...you've seen what he's capable of."

I tried not to shudder from the electric tickle of his breath. "Okay, but I still think we should go sit down."

Alex didn't look happy, but we still ended up in the living room. The seating arrangement proved to be a difficult task, since Alex didn't want me sitting next to Nicholas, but I thought it wouldn't be a good idea to sit by Alex, considering what the consequences could be. I was realizing very quickly that, if it turned out to be true—if Alex and I being close to one another for too long could end up killing us—then there might be a huge problem because we seemed to magnetize toward each other.

Finally Alex sat down beside Nicholas, and I shared a sofa with Aislin.

Alex jumped to the point immediately. "Alright, start talking."

"About what?" Nicholas pressed back a grin. "What do you want me to tell you?"

Afraid Alex might hit him again, I chimed in. "How about you tell us what happened on the beach."

Nicholas stared at me with a twinkle in his golden eyes. "That would be an example of how extraordinary you are."

"Okay..." Let the running around in circles begin. "Define why that makes me extraordinary."

47

Nicholas flexed his hand and winced. "Well…that makes you extraordinary because you erased a vision. Which, might I add, is something that's completely forbidden and could have severe consequences." His eyes darkened. "If I wanted to, I could turn you into the Foreseers…you know there's punishment for erasing visions."

"What kind of a punishment?" I asked curiously, thinking of my father and the strange place he was in.

"I don't know for sure…." Nicholas paused, tapping his finger on his lips. "I've only heard of one Foreseer being punished for erasing a vision."

"Do you know who he is?" I leaned forward, anxious to hear his answer.

He shook his head. "Our kind doesn't like to talk about things like that because…well, I think because it reminds everyone of how much control and power Foreseer's really have."

I got up and grabbed the crystal ball from off the desk. "So can you explain to me what this is?" I asked, taking a seat back on the sofa.

"Where did you get that?" Nicholas' eyes sparkled in the glittering purple glow of the crystal ball.

"That's not important," I told him and balanced the crystal ball on the coffee table. "What's important is that you tell me what it is."

Nicholas slowly reached for the crystal ball, hesitating, before picking it up. I saw Alex tense up and I tensed up too since I didn't know what the crystal ball did. For all I knew, it held enough power to destroy us all; something that should probably not be held by a very tricky faerie/Foreseer.

He stared at the crystal ball in awe for a moment, and then set it back on the coffee table. "That," he pointed at the crystal ball, "is what we Foreseer's refer to as a mapping ball. They're very rare to come by—in fact, they're almost nonexistent."

"So what does a mapping ball do?" I asked.

Nicholas furrowed his eyebrows at the mapping ball. "It holds a map of someone's life. It shows all the decisions they've made...although, some mapping balls are used to keep a secret hidden in the midst of thousands of their memories. It really is the most amazing thing..." He glanced up at me. "So whose is it?"

I caught Alex's eye, wondering if I should divulge this bit of information to Nicholas. Alex's expression was serious, which meant he didn't want me to say anything.

"There's no use trying to keep it from me," Nicholas said. "Because I'm sure you're going to want to know how to use it, and that means you and I are going to have to go inside it."

Well, okay then. I tore my gaze off Alex. "It's my father's."

Nicholas gaped at me. "I thought you told me you didn't know who your father is."

"I just recently discovered his identity," I explained, purposely being vague.

"What!" Aislin cried out, scaring the crap out of everyone, including me—I think we all had forgot she was there. "Why didn't anyone tell me....any of this?"

I shook my head at Alex. "Didn't you explain this to her while I was sleeping?"

"You were already all wound up about Laylen," Alex explained to Aislin. "So I thought I would spare you the burden."

Tears dripped from her eyes. "You could have told me."

As much as I hated when people kept things from other people, I think Alex might have been on the right track with this one.

"So," I turned my attention back to Nicholas, figuring it was best to move on, "about the mapping ball. How do we get inside it?"

"How did you manage to find out who your father was?" Nicholas asked, ignoring my question. "And how did you get a hold of his mapping ball?"

"My mom gave it to me," I lied.

He leaned back in the sofa and rested his arms behind his head. "You managed to save her then?"

I was kind of surprised he didn't know this already, since we created such an uproar during our escaped from The Underworld. "Yeah, and without your help I might add."

"Well, I wouldn't say that." He grinned at me. "Seeing as how you got the Ira from me."

"After you kidnapped me and chained me to the wall," I snapped.

"So what's the purpose of the mapping ball?" Alex interrupted, picking up the mapping ball and examining it over.

Nicholas rolled his eyes. "I already told you it's to keep track of the things someone has done in their lifetime." He nodded at the mapping ball. "If that is your dad's, then when we go inside it, we should be able to follow a map of his life."

Alex's forehead creased over. "Why would your dad give this to you?" he asked me.

"I thought you said your mom gave it to you." Nicholas leaned forward, a look of intrigue rising on his face.

I shot Alex a way-to-go look; it was not like Alex to be so careless. "My dad said it would tell me how to save the world from Stephan and his deadly minions." I paused, the wheels in my head turning. "If it holds a map of his life, then maybe I can see what vision he erased and recreated to make it so Stephan could end the world." I looked at Nicholas, curious to see how he reacted to what I said.

He clapped his hands. "Bravo on figuring that one out."

"You knew that already?" I asked, getting pissed off.

He shrugged. "I know a lot of things I don't choose to share."

"But you didn't say anything and you have to—you made a Blood Promise." I shot Alex a worried look, wondering what happened, but he looked just as lost as me.

"They're called loopholes, Gemma," Nicholas informed me with a pleased grin. "You have to ask me the question in order for me to tell you what I know."

There are always loopholes—my mother told me this once. "Okay, so do you know how to fix all of this then?" I asked. "Do you know what I need to do?"

Nicholas smile was all trickery. "I do. Would you like me tell you?"

Freaking faeries. "Yes. I am asking you to please share everything that you know about mapping balls and Stephan's evil plan."

Aislin's cell phone rang from inside the pocket of her khaki shorts. She took it out and glanced down at the screen. "Whose number is that?" She got to her feet. "Hello?" she said into her phone as she walked out of the room.

I turned my attention back to Nicholas. "So what do you know?"

"What do I know...Well, for starters that little buzzing connection you two have is going to kill you if you can't tone it down, " Nicholas said, clearly amused with himself. My face fell as he continued, "It's not necessarily your closeness that will do it, though, so much as making that little connection of yours heat up. The more the electricity flows between you two, the more energy the star loses and

52

the more energy you two lose. And if you lose too much, you both die."

"How do you know all this?" I stammered. "How do you even know about the electricity?" Hardly anyone knew about that.

"Stephan informed me when he marked me." He glared down at the black triangle tracing the red symbol tattooed on his arm.

"But how does Stephan even know about our connection?" I glanced at Alex. "Did you tell him?"

Alex shook his head. "I didn't tell him..." His gaze wandered to the doorway of the kitchen. "Dammit, Aislin."

Aislin peeked out, the phone still pressed to her ear. "What?"

Alex scowled at her. "You told Stephan about the electricity?"

Aislin pulled an oh-crap face. "I'm on the phone," she hissed and ducked back into the kitchen.

I took a deep breath, struggling to keep my composure contained. "So if we can control the electricity and keep it to a bare minimum, then we won't die?"

Nicholas raised an eyebrow skeptically. "Can you control it?"

I met Alex's eyes, and sparks instantly crackled like a wildfire. Could we control it? Maybe...if we could keep our emotions and intense looks contained.

"I think we might be able to," I said, my eyes locked on Alex, who seemed to be waiting for my answer.

"Of course we can," he said, as if it were the easiest thing in the world. Lucky him, because I had a feeling it was going to be difficult. At least for me it was.

"So we go inside the mapping ball, find out what vision my dad changed and then what?" I asked. "I mean, I still don't get how I erased and recreated what happened to me on the beach...I mean there was two of me."

"That's where everything becomes tricky." Nicholas grabbed the mapping ball from Alex's hands, got up, and walked toward me. Alex started to get to his feet, but I shook my head, telling him to stay put. "You see, the thing about visions," Nicholas sat down on the couch beside me, "is that everything is connected to each other."

I scooted away from him. "I'm not sure what you mean."

Nicholas stared down at the mapping ball. "In the Foreseer world, every vision is connected."

"Okay..." Where was he going with this?

Sensing my confusion, he explained further. "Say you make the decision to become a singer; so, you go down to the local talent show and try out, win, and go on to become a famous singer."

"But I can't sing," I told him, even though I knew he was talking hypothetically.

He flashed me an annoyed look as he went on, "Each one of those events that took place would be their own vision. The decision, the trying out, and the winning—all of them led to you becoming famous."

"I still don't get what you're saying."

"I'm saying they're all connected to one another—each one had to happen in order for the other one to happen."

Ding. The light bulb in my head finally turned on. "So if I never made the decision to become a singer, then none of the rest would have happened."

"Exactly," Nicholas said. "And if a Foreseer wanted to change your life, he could just alter the first event and it could change everything from that point on. Say he put the idea in your head to become a ballerina, and on your way to trying out, you left a minute later because you had to put on your tutu. And because you left one minute later you get in a car accident and die."

Yeah, like I would ever wear a tutu. "But how could changing what I wanted to be, change my life that much?"

"Haven't you ever heard of the butterfly effect?" he asked.

"Vaguely," I replied.

"Well, it's like that," Nicholas explained. "Change one small thing in your life and it can greatly affect the rest of it." He paused, mulling something over. "I'm not sure what your father erased and recreated in order to get the world to end, but in order for us to stop it without doing more damage, the best thing to do is to erase him before he changes it."

55

"What?" I gaped at him. "Erase my dad?"

"Not in the sense of erasing your actual father." Nicholas said. "We would go into the mapping ball, find the memory of your father where he changed the vision, and erase him before he does it…like you did with yourself on the beach."

I was kind of getting it now. "Okay, so we go into the mapping ball, filled with all of my dad's memories of his life, find the one where he changed the world's future, and I place a hand on him and erase him before he does?"

Nicholas nodded. "Pretty much, yes."

"And how are we supposed to find the memory? I mean it could take forever."

Nicholas smiled, tapping the side of his head. "The answers are in here."

I frowned. "In your head?"

He winked at me. "In yours."

My dad had also said this, but what did it mean? "Can you please explain what that means?"

"I will when we get in there," he said simply.

I sighed, hoping he wasn't toying with me. "And what if the vision my father changed is still bad?" I asked, casting a glance at Alex. I'm not sure why, but I suddenly thought of the vision I kept having, where he and I were at the lake and the light smothered us.

"It doesn't matter. It's how things were—or, are supposed to be." Nicholas traced the Foreseers' mark circling his wrist. "Despite how powerful some of us get, Foreseers

56

are only supposed to see visions, not change them or control them to our liking."

At that moment, Nicholas actual seemed like a good person who cared about the world. It was weird seeing him like that, all serious and somewhat normal.

My father, on the other hand, seemed like the opposite. He had changed a vision so the world would end in the most horrible way. Everything would freeze over and all the witches, fey, vampires, and Death Walkers connected to Malefiscus would run the streets killing everyone.

"So how do we get inside the mapping ball?" I asked. The sooner we put everything back together, the sooner we could all have a normal life...at least, I hope that's what waited for us in the future.

"That's the tricky part," he said.

I rubbed my forehead, which was throbbing from the stress. "You've already said that like twice."

"Well, this one's tricky as well." He spun the mapping ball around in his hand. "This thing uses a lot of power."

I pointed at myself. "Like the power of a unique Foreseer."

He shook his head. "More power than even you have. We need the power of the main crystal ball that all the other crystal balls run off."

My mouth slipped to a frown as I remembered the giant crystal ball that sucked its energy away from people. I peeked over at Alex and shuttered at the mental image of him strapped to the crystal with tubes embedded into his skin.

"So, we what? Just take the mapping ball there and use the crystal ball's power?" I asked.

Nicholas looked down at his hand. "We bring it back," he said, opening and closing his hand.

"Bring it back?" I glanced at Nicholas' hand. What was he doing? "And how do we do that?"

"You think I'm actually going to let you go off to the City of Crystal alone with her," Alex interrupted.

"Well, you could always let me go by myself and hope I'll come back," Nicholas remarked, trying to get under Alex's skin.

"Alex," I said. "You've got to stop. Let me handle this. It's what I'm supposed to do."

Alex suddenly looked horrified. "I'm not going to let you go off alone with him." He got up and pulled me up with him. He took me over to the corner of the living room and lowered his voice, his eyes pressing. "Don't forget what he did to you, just because you erased it."

"I understand where you're coming from—I really do—but you've got to stop worrying about me all the time. I'm not a girl who needs to be protected by you because she has a star's energy that will save the world. I'm a girl with a very unique Foreseer gift, who needs to save the world from the star's energy."

Alex ran his fingers though his hair as he stared off into empty space. "How am I supposed to just stop doing something, when it's all I want to do?"

My heart thumped insanely in my chest and, when he looked at me, I just about stopped breathing.

"Yeah, I give you two like a day before you end up killing one another," Nicholas' laughter-filled voice intruded on our moment.

I scowled at Nicholas. "Thanks for your opinion," I said sarcastically. "But we'll be fine." Although, I wasn't sure I believed my own words.

"Sure you will," Nicholas' grin was mocking.

"We have a problem," Aislin announced as she entered the room.

"Of course we do," Alex said with an eye roll. "The world is going to end unless we fix it."

She shook her head quickly. "No, not that problem... Your mom just called from a payphone and told me Laylen's in trouble."

"What kind of trouble?" The pitch of my voice was startlingly high.

"He's..." She trailed off, giving a wary glance at Nicholas. "Maybe we should discuss this in private."

"Why? He can't go anywhere," I pointed out, but she was still hesitant, and I found myself bursting with aggravation. "Just say whatever it is."

"He's at..." She lowered her voice. "He was at the Red Dragon."

"Please don't tell me that's another club," I grimaced.

Silence and my heart sank,

"Oh, it's a club," Alex said. "An exclusive club for anyone and anything that has a thirst for the evil side."

"Like the Black Dungeon?" I asked.

He shook his head. "It's much worse."

Oh my God! I couldn't breathe. "But if there are vampires at this club, they might kill him because he killed Vladislav."

"Would you two shut up!" Aislin cried, practically spitting in our faces. "I said he was at the Red Dragon, but someone we know picked him up from there."

"Who?" I asked at the same time Alex said, "Great. Just what we need."

I gave him a funny look. "Do you know who picked him up?"

Alex squirmed uncomfortably and tucked his hands into his pockets. "Yeah, I think might."

"I mean, I know she lives close by here and everything," Aislin said, looking hurt. "But I just never thought Laylen would contact her."

"Who the heck is this 'her'?" I wanted to know.

Aislin glanced at Alex, her eyes pushing for him to explain, but he stayed mute, as he stared down at the floor.

"It's Stasha." Aislin sighed. "She used to be a Keeper—well, I guess she technically still is, but she…decided she didn't want to be part of the circle anymore."

"Sounds like a smart girl to me," I remarked.

"Yeah..." Her gaze flicked in Alex's direction. "She kind of left because of him."

"Why would she leave because of him?" I asked, noticing how much more uncomfortable Alex was getting.

Nicholas stood up and suddenly he was right next to me. "Because she and Alex used to be *lovers*, but since he's emotionally dead inside, he broke her heart," he teased, pouting out his bottom lip.

I almost slapped him. I don't know why, though. He was just telling me the truth. But the truth hurt in a way I had never felt before—the prickle was confirming it. Really, it shouldn't bother me that Alex once had a girlfriend—hello, he's twenty years old—but still...it was bugging the crap out of me.

Everyone had their eyes on me, watching me as if they were waiting for me to flip out. I, however, stayed cool, calm, and collected, at least on the outside.

"So what do we do?" I asked, my voice smoothing out like honey. "Do we call Laylen? Or do we need to go get him? And is this Stasha girl keeping an eye on him?"

Aislin suddenly looked a bit on the jittery side. "Your mom didn't say anything about that. She just said she found him standing outside the Red Dragon talking to Stasha, and when she went to go get him, he took off with her."

"Is my mom heading back here?" I asked her.

Aislin looked at Alex anxiously, which puzzled him as much as it did me. "Yeah...I think she is."

61

"What, you don't know if she is?" I asked.

Aislin shook her head way too quickly. "No, she is."

"What are you—"

"I think we should go get Laylen," she announced over me. "I think he needs someone right now, and Stasha probably isn't the best person for him to be around."

"Why? What's wrong with her?" I asked in an unintentionally rude tone.

"There's nothing wrong with her." Alex was watching me in a way that made me feel really vulnerable, as if he could see my jealousy written all over me. "But Aislin's probably right. Stasha can be a little on the…unsympathetic side, and that's probably the last thing Laylen needs right now."

"I still can't believe Halfy finally went off the deep end," Nicholas laughed.

"He didn't go off the deep end!" I screamed for reasons that were unknown. The prickle went insane, poking and stabbing and eating away at the back of my neck. "And it's my fault he…wants to drink blood."

"Why?" Nicholas asked, tapping his fingers together as if I we were discussing something scandalous. "What did you *do*?"

He was getting on my nerves, so I pinched his arm. He let out a yelp, but then grinned. "You know, I swear you get feistier by the second."

"Well, you bring it out of me," I said snidely. He opened his mouth to say something, but I talked over him. "So how far is Stasha's house? Close, I hope."

"Not too far," Aislin said, glancing at the clock on her cellphone. "Probably about a thirty-minute drive."

"I don't think we should all go," Alex told Aislin. "There are a lot of us, and besides, you know how she is."

"But I don't know how she is," I pointed out.

He ignored me. "So should we hit the road?"

We were not going back to *that* again. "You didn't answer my question."

He let out an aggravated sigh. "You remember when I told you that some Keepers have gifts, like Sophia's gift of…" He trailed off, looking guilty for bringing up my soul detachment.

"Yeah, I remember." I tried not to sound bitter.

"Well, Stasha has a gift too." He rubbed the back of his neck tensely. "She has the gift of…death."

"Like she kills people or something?" I asked with a shiver.

"Not for fun," Alex clarified. "She just can, you know, kill if she wants to."

I cringed. "Everyone can kill if they want to, Alex."

"Yeah, but not like she can," he said. "She can kill with her touch."

"So she can kill me if she touches me?" I asked.

"Only if she wants to."

Well, that sounded lovely. And I had this creepy feeling she might end up wanting to.

"Oh, my God." Aislin's green eyes widened as she looked at us fearfully. "You don't think that Laylen went there to drink the blood of someone Stasha killed."

Alex didn't answer and I felt my stomach churn.

"No—no, he wouldn't," I stuttered, but honestly I wasn't sure. Urgency spilled through the air. "I think we should all go get him. NOW!"

Alex shook his head. "I don't think you should go."

"I don't really care what you think," I snapped. "I'm going. Laylen needs me."

"I'm going to see if I can go get a hold of Stasha and let her know we're coming," Aislin talked over us. She opened her phone and stepped into the hallway.

"You shouldn't go." Alex's voice was less demanding and more begging.

"I need to," I told him. "Laylen needs me, and this is all my fault anyway."

"She won't like you being there," he mumbled, frustrated.

"Who? Stasha?" I asked curiously. "Why?"

"Because…she just won't." He was looking at me strangely.

The sly look on Nicholas' face meant he was about to say something unpleasant. "He doesn't want you there because he's afraid Stasha will try to kill you."

"But I haven't done anything to her," I grimaced.

64

"Oh, but you have." He patted Alex on the back. "This one right here broke her heart."

Alex smacked his arm away and his eyes lit up with fury. "Keep your mouth shut."

"Yeah, well, his breaking her heart has nothing to do with me," I told Nicholas. "I wasn't even there."

"Oh, but it does have to do with you." There was a mischievous sparkle in the faerie's golden eyes. "Like I said, Stasha was madly in love with him."

"Shut the hell up," Alex growled, clenching his hand into fists.

But Nicholas continued on unbothered. "But since he is emotionally hollow, he broke her heart, of course."

"Of course." I rolled my eyes at him, because he was being annoying. Well, a little annoying. I had to admit it did make me feel slightly better that Alex broke her heart, not the other way around. "But that doesn't explain why she'll want to kill me. I didn't make him break her heart."

"She'll want to kill you because she'll see how you two look at one another." He smirked. "Your desire for each other is ridiculously obvious."

Why, oh why, did Nicholas get a sick twisted pleasure on making things awkward? I mean, was it a faerie thing? Or was it just him? I shifted uncomfortably and so did Alex.

"No, it's not," I tried to assure Nicholas, but my voice failed me.

"Yes it is—it shows in your eyes." He touched the corner of my eye with his finger and I flinched back.

"Don't touch her ever again," Alex said, getting in his face.

"Alright, let's just stop," I said, deciding to be the peace maker. "Now I understand your concern," I told Alex. "About your ex-girlfriend wanting to kill me or whatever, but I'm sure I'll be fine."

Alex opened his mouth to protest, and I questioned if there was some other reason he didn't want me to go. Those other reasons ate away at my insides.

"I think she should go with us," Aislin said from the hallway.

Daggers shot from Alex's bright green eyes. "Well, no one asked for your opinion."

"And no one asked for yours," she snapped, shutting her cellphone. "You can go. You're right—Laylen needs you." She paused, looking pained. "You seem to understand him better than anyone...and he trusts you."

It hurt her to say it, and I realized Aislin wasn't that bad. Sure, she had done some things in her past that weren't that great, but, like Alex, she probably was under the control of her father.

"So, we should get going." Aislin grabbed the car keys from off the desk. "Stasha didn't answer her phone, so we're just going to have to surprise them."

"Wait? What about my mom?" I asked. "She'll wonder where we are."

66

"We'll leave her a note," Aislin said quickly. "Besides, I think she needed to go somewhere—to the store. She was going to the store to pick up some food."

Okay...she was acting weird. I pointed a finger at Nicholas. "Well, what are we going to do with him?"

Alex rubbed his jawline as he deliberated this. "We could tie him back up in the garage."

"Oh, that would be nice," I said, crossing my arms. "My mom showing up and finding him tied up in the garage." I paused. "I think we should take him. Besides, if someone shows up here, he'll tell them everything—you know he will."

Alex knew I was right, but he still didn't look very happy. "Fine, he can come."

We hid the mapping ball and locked up the house, with both locks and magical charms. Then we headed down the desolate highway, toward the next town where Stasha lived. Night had blanketed over the land, the moon shining at its fullest. Silver and purple stars twinkled a soft lullaby, the ocean purring along with the tune.

The inside of the car was absurdly hot, due to both the humid air and the electricity. I didn't know what it was about cars, but it brought out the heat between Alex and I. Thankfully, he was driving and I was in the backseat, sitting next to Nicholas, who was practically like an air freshener with how much rainy-flower scent flowed off him. I couldn't breathe, and finally I had to roll down the window. The air pumped oxygen through my lungs, and I breathed in its salty scent with a deep, lingering breath.

"You doing okay back there?"

I tore myself away from the window and found Alex watching me in the rearview mirror.

"Yeah, it's just a little hot back here." I fanned myself with my hand.

Nicholas let out a loud snore. He had dozed off the minute we pulled out of the driveway. Aislin had nodded off too, not too shortly after the town had disappeared from our view. Evidently, everyone was tired.

"It is hot in here," he agreed.

The pale glow of the moon trickled inside the cab of the car, lighting his hands clutched tightly on the steering-wheel.

"Maybe you should roll your window down too," I suggested, hoping to pump in some more circulation. God, what had I been thinking, climbing in here with him?

"Good idea." He rolled down his window and a gentle breeze lulled in. It helped…a little.

"Make-up Smeared Eyes" by Automatic Loveletter hummed from the speakers, and between the soft beat of the music and the gentle breeze, I found myself getting drowsy.

I yawned, my head feeling heavy.

"Are you tired?" he asked, glancing at the bright red numbers on the clock.

"Yeah, a little."

"You should get some rest," he said in a soft voice. "You need to be awake when we get there."

And suddenly I was wide awake. I leaned forward in the chair. "I don't get it...You act like this Stasha is...like going to murder me or something."

"No, she's not that bad, but..." He paused. "But she has jealousy issues."

Ah, the emotion of jealousy. I've experienced that one a few times, and I can't say I'm a fan.

"If she's like that, then why did you date her?" I regretted the words as soon as they left my mouth.

He shifted in the seat uncomfortably. "That's why I dated her...It was easy not to feel things with her...unlike with some people." His eyes met mine in the mirror and the look he gave me made my body tingle.

Stop thinking about him like that. Just stop.

I bit at my nails. "I think we should —"

Suddenly, a shadowy figure appeared in the road. I let out a screamed as Alex slammed on the breaks. Tires roared. The car lurched forward...crunching...a bright light...yellow eyes...then blackness.

Chapter 7

I had never felt this kind of pain before. Never. It was like my body was compressed into a ball, my bones breaking and conforming to fit the position. It hurt so bad…so bad…

"Gemma."

Who said that?

"Gemma, can you hear?"

I knew that voice. It was the most wonderful voice in the world.

I forced my eyes open and saw the beautiful boy staring down at me with the brightest green eyes I had ever seen.

"Are you alright?" the boy asked. Stars danced behind him. They were pretty.

I told my head to nod, but it didn't. There was gravel in my hair and my skin was sticky and warm.

A girl appeared above me. I knew her too. Blood stained her golden brown hair.

"Look." She pointed at my stomach.

The boy's eyes widened and with one swift movement, he swooped me up in his arms.

"Get us out of here," the boy yelled to the girl. "Now!"

She looked at him helplessly. "Where do you expect me to take us?"

"To Stasha's." There was panic on the boy's face, and I wanted to tell him it would be okay—everything would be okay—but I couldn't. "You have your crystal, right?"

She nodded. "But what about him?" She pointed down at the ground.

There was sadness in the boy's eyes. "We'll have to leave him here....If we don't get her out of here...she might not make it. Besides, you know they pick up their own."

"Alright." The girl looked so sad. "Let's go then."

The boy said something else to me, but I couldn't hear it; I could only see his lips moving.

My eyelids were heavy, so I shut them.

I was dying. I don't know how I knew, but I just knew: this was what death felt like. There was no pain, no anguish, no burden of the star. Everything felt complete, except for one thing. A piece of me was missing. Not an actual piece per se, but something I was connected to—electrically connected to. Alex. I needed Alex.

This empty feeling choked up inside me. I tried to open my eyes, to see where I was, but I couldn't. Then came the voice. A voice I knew vaguely—my father's voice.

"You can't give up," he whispered. "You need to fix my mistakes."

They're your mistakes, so you fix them, I wanted to say, but I couldn't speak. In fact I wasn't even sure I had a mouth anymore.

"*You can do it, my Gemma," he said. "I know you can.*"

But what if I can't?

"*Now open your eyes," he commanded. "Today is not the day you're going to die, Gemma Lucas.*"

Why was he always saying this to me? Did he even know when my death would come?

My eyelids slowly lifted open. Light. Alex and me by the lake. Hugging. Ice everywhere.

Why did it always come back to this?

The bright light carried me away.

The first thing I was aware of was that I was lying in a very soft bed, like I had fallen asleep in a pile of feathers. The next thing I noticed was how bad my body hurt, like every bone in my body had snapped in two. My stomach was in the most pain, like someone had drilled a hole in it.

I finally willed my eyelids to open. The light stung at my eyes and I blinked several times as I slowly sat up.

"Oh, God." I hunched over and cradled my arm around my stomach, trying not to cry out in pain. I lifted the bottom of my blood-stained t-shirt and saw a very large section of my stomach was bandaged over. I sifted through my memories, trying to remember. "What happened?"

"We got in a car accident." Alex's voice startled me. He was standing in the doorway, tired bags under his eyes, his hair a mess and not in an intentional way. There was something in his expression that I couldn't quite place; tiredness...pain...or maybe it was vulnerability.

He stepped cautiously into the room, which I now noticed was overwhelmed with plants. Yes, plants. They were everywhere. On shelves, on the dresser; there were even leafy vines dangling from the olive-colored ceiling.

"What is this place?" I asked, staring up at the vines.

He sat down on the foot of the bed, keeping some distance between us. "It's Stasha's...the plants are good for her gift."

I pulled a face. "Oh, yippy." I shifted my body weight and the muscles of my stomach tightened. I winced. "So, we were in a car accident?"

He arched an eyebrow at me. "You don't remember?"

I shook my head. "Not really. I mean, kind of...I remember the thing in the road."

"That thing in the road was a Death Walker."

I tensed. "Was—does that mean—"

"No, it was just a stray." He shrugged. "It happens sometimes....one that's gotten lost from the pack."

They sounded like wolves.

I nodded and pointed at my stomach. "So what happened here?"

He took an unsteady breath as if the memory upset him. "A piece of glass cut you." He brushed his finger across my hairline. "You also hit your head."

"It felt like I was dying," I said softly as I touched the tender spot on my head.

Fear filled his eyes. "You were."

I sat on that for a moment, frozen in shock. "But I didn't?" I asked it as a question. A very stupid question. Obviously I wasn't dead. "Is everyone else okay?" I asked.

He didn't answer, staring straight ahead at the wall.

"Is everyone okay?" I repeated in a panic.

Still nothing.

"It's not Aislin…" My voice quivered and tears stung at my eyes.

"No, it's not Aislin," he said hurriedly. "She's fine."

"Well, then, what is it? I can tell something's wrong, so just tell me," I pleaded.

He ran his fingers through his hair. "It's Nicholas…he's dead."

Chapter 8

At first I wasn't sure I heard him right.

Dead?

Dead.

Nicholas is dead.

What was I supposed to do with this?

"Are you alright?" Alex asked me after my silence became almost maddening.

"I...I don't know." I took in the feeling that was poking at my neck. What was this—this horrible, wretched, awful sickness building up in my body? I gripped tightly at the blankets, wishing desperately that the pain would go away. *Go away. Go away.* "How did he—he die?"

Alex swallowed hard. "When we hit the Death Walker, it threw the car into a telephone pole...he didn't make it."

"But I did," I whispered.

Alex's eyes were wide. "But you shouldn't have....You shouldn't be here, Gemma..." He looked like he was about in tears and it was kind of freaking me out. I have never seen so much emotion pour out of those bright green eyes before. "You almost...you almost died."

Breathe, breathe, breathe.

He stared down at the hardwood floor, breathing loudly, as he mumbled to himself, "one minute you were dying and then suddenly you weren't. God, what if you hadn't made it."

I thought of the words my father whispered to me. "'Today is not the day you're going to die.'" I suddenly wondered if maybe my dad knew when my death day was.

Alex's head whipped over to me. "What?"

Whoops. I did not mean to say that out loud. "That's what I heard when I...when I was dying. 'Today is not the day you're going to die.'" I paused. "It was my father's voice."

"You heard your father?" he asked, stunned.

I nodded. "He also reminded me that I needed to fix his mistakes." Was that why I was still here? Was that why I didn't die?

I thought of Nicholas and how fixing my dad's mistakes no longer seemed possible. How was I supposed to go into the mapping ball without him?

The thought of Nicholas made my stomach lurch. Yes, he had been slightly obnoxious, he teased me to no end, and he did things that could be considered evil, but only because he was marked with the Mark of Malefiscus.

My stomach churned again and suddenly I knew...

I was going to puke.

I jumped up, ignoring the pain in my stomach. "Where's the bathroom?"

Alex, looking mystified, pointed over his shoulder. "There's one right there."

I ran over to the door and threw it open.

"Gemma, what's wrong?" Alex asked worriedly, getting to his feet.

I slammed the door shut, ran over to the toilet, and puked until my stomach was empty.

Chapter 9

I'm going to spare you the nasty details of the rest of my puking experience.

All I can say was it was gross.

And it didn't make me feel better. At all.

After I rinsed my mouth and splashed my face with cold water, I stared at my reflection in the mirror. I looked like crap, I really did. My eyes were red and swollen, my skin was paler than normal. There was a small cut on my forehead, right below my hairline.

My violet eyes stared back at me accusingly. This was my fault. I should have let Alex tie him up in the garage; he would have been better off.

"Everything is my fault," I whispered at my reflection.

Someone banged on the door and I jumped back. "Yeah."

"You okay in there?" Alex's cautious voice floated through the door.

"Yeah...." My reflection was laughing at me. I took a deep breath and pulled myself together the best that I could and opened the door. "I'm just not feeling very well."

He nodded, giving me a look of understanding. "Do you want to lie down?"

I shook my head. "I want to see Laylen. Is he okay?"

He frowned at my question. "He's fine, I guess."

"Well, can I see him?" I asked, wishing he would stop giving me that look. It was a look that was a mix between annoyance, hurt, and disappointment. It was a look that made me feel guilty for something I should not feel guilty about.

"Yeah, you can see him." His tone was guarded. "He's out there." He nodded his head at the door.

"Thanks," I muttered as I stepped past him.

He followed me out of the room and down the hallway, keeping his distance. The air smelled very planty, to the point that it almost made me gag. I held back my gag. My stomach was still weak, and I didn't want to puke all over the nice hardwood floor.

The hallway led to a living room that had olive green walls painted with a rosy pattern. A set of rose embroidered sofas centered the room, along with a coffee table. Like the bedroom, there were plants all over the walls, the shelves, and the vines dangling from the ceiling were detailed with tiny pink flowers.

I glanced over my shoulder at Alex and raised my eyebrows. "Really?"

"The plants help her gift," he said defensively. "The oxygen's good for her or something...I don't know."

I pressed my lips together to keep from saying anything further. Jealousy was an ugly color, and I was not going to let it shine all over me.

"I think everyone's in the kitchen." Alex pointed to our right.

I walked to the kitchen doorway and Alex caught my arm. "Hey...." He seemed to be struggling for words. Finally he said, "You're feeling okay, right?"

"Yeah, I..." All words suddenly left me because, out of the corner of my eyes, I caught sight of a blond-haired, blue-tipped banged, blue-eyed vampire sitting at the table. I just about ran over to him and gave him a big hug. I wasn't sure where the feeling came from. I mean, I could try to figure it out, but sometimes feelings weren't easy to solve.

He was not alone at the table. Aislin was also there, her golden-brown hair damp like she just got out of the shower. Her eyes were swollen and tear-stained. She was wearing different clothes and the pink floral dress she had on was girly even for her.

The other person at the table was also dressed in a floral dress, just a different color. Her blonde hair reminded me of sunshine and sunflowers and her eyes were a bright blue. Tan leather gloves covered her hands. I had seen this girl before, in a photo back at Laylen's house; a photo in which this girl was clearly dating Alex.

I hated this girl.

I really did.

Okay, maybe I should use the word dislike.

From the dark look she shot me, I could tell she hated—or disliked—me too.

"Everything okay?" she asked, looking through me, right at Alex.

"Everything's fine, Stasha," he answered, walking past me.

Stasha gave me the death stare, so I looked away at Laylen, who was fiddling with his lip ring, which I was beginning to notice was something he did while he was in deep thought.

He caught my eye and he looked the slightest bit relieved. Then, without saying a word, he stood up and came over to me. Everyone was watching us, so I took his hand and pulled him into the living room, out of the watchful gaze of all their eyes. Particularly Alex's, which I could feel burning into me, even through the wall.

Neither of us spoke. I wasn't sure what to say to him. This was the second time he had run away, and I was beginning to worry one of these times I wouldn't find him.

"Are you okay?" I finally asked.

He didn't answer right away. "I don't know."

"You had me worried," I told him truthfully.

"I know," he said. "I'm sorry. I just freaked out when your mom told me this was done on purpose to me...I didn't do anything, though...I didn't bite anyone."

"You could have talked to me," I said. "Instead of running away."

81

He took a shaky breath. "You have your own problems."

"It doesn't matter," I said. "I'll always be there for you, just like you are for me."

He let out a relieved breath as if he had been waiting for me to say those exact words.

"You and I are in this together." I looked him straight in the eye. "Promise me you won't run away again."

He took my hand and gave it a squeeze. "Okay. We're in this together."

About ten minutes later, we were getting ready to leave. Which was a good thing, at least for me, since nine out of those ten minutes, Stasha gave me the stink eye. It made me extremely uneasy and for some reason, I kept thinking of Edgar Allan Poe's "The Tell-Tale Heart."

We were transporting back to the beach house, which I was thankful for. The last thing I wanted to do right now was get in a moving vehicle. Even though the Chevy Tahoe was a monstrous beast, it still took quite the beating when it had rammed into the Death Walker and the telephone pole.

All five of us were sitting in Stasha's living room. Aislin had her candle lit and crystal in hand. I went to take my necklace off, to avoid repelling Aislin's magic back on her, when I realized it was missing.

"Oh, no." I touched my neck, panicking. "Where's my necklace?"

"Calm down," Alex said. "I took it off when Aislin transported us here. I left it on the nightstand in the room you were in."

I nodded and headed off to the bedroom, but the necklace wasn't on the night stand. I searched the bedroom floor, in the bed, under the bed. I even checked the bathroom I puked my guts out in. But nothing. No necklace.

Okay, so I really didn't want to be the girl who cried over losing a piece of jewelry, but I was going to be if I didn't find it.

"Crap," I muttered with a light stomp of my foot.

"Looking for this?"

I spun around. Stasha. She was standing just inside the doorway, her glove-covered hand up in front of her, something shiny and silver dangling from her finger.

"Why do you have that?" I asked, reaching to take the necklace.

She pulled her hand back. "I wasn't giving it back to you."

Okay, I had a feeling this was going to be fun. "Please give it back?" I asked, trying to keep my tone as polite sounding as possible.

With a sardonic grin on her face, she shook her head and I was unexpectedly reminded of Kelsey Merritt, a girl I used to go to school with who loved to torture me. Of course Stasha was a little different, seeing how she could kill me with her touch.

"I know girls like you." She strutted into the room, swinging the necklace around on her finger. "Sad. Lonely. *Pathetic*. God, I can't believe Alex would even have the slightest bit of interest in you."

Alright, so in the past, I had let girls like Stasha walk over me, but today was different—I was different. Honestly, I just wanted to shove her down. So I did. She looked shocked as she fell backward toward the floor and landed on her butt. I seized the opportunity to snatch the necklace away from her. Then, I ran like hell. I was not stupid enough to stick around and face the wrath of a girl who could kill me simply by touching me. But I didn't make it very far down the hall before something wrapped around my ankle and yanked me flat on my face. I kicked my leg, thinking I would nail her in the head, but I didn't hit anything.

I glanced behind me and realized it was not Stasha that knocked me to the floor. It was…well, it was the freaky plant vines that dangled from the ceiling. They were alive or something.

Stasha walked slowly toward me, and I opened my mouth to scream, but another vine wrapped around my mouth, silencing any noise from escaping. She knelt down in front of me and leaned into my face.

"You should know better than to mess with someone like me," she whispered, pulling off one of her gloves.

She should know better than to mess with me, I thought, wishing I could say it out loud, but couldn't because of the vine's death-grip around my mouth.

She reached her deathly hand toward me, ready to touch me, ready to kill. Crazy lunatic. How could Alex have dated this nut job?

I shut my eyes, and formed a mental picture of the beach just outside the beach house, just enough of a distance away that the *Praesidium* wouldn't get in my way. I could hear the ocean waves crashing onto the sandy shore. I could see the moon beaming down from the sky. I could feel the salty air kissing against my cheeks.

"What are you doing?" Stasha asked, her voice muffled.

I kept my eyes shut, focusing on the picture. "Take me there," I whispered, and I could almost feel the sand in my toes.

But then a hand grabbed my arm and I felt nothing but fire.

Chapter 10

My face smacked against the sand. I scrambled to my feet and ran over to the ocean. My arm was burning up — it had to be on fire. But there were no flames on my skin.

I dunked my arm into the salty water, expecting relief, but instead getting more pain. I let out a jaw-clenched scream, and ran for the beach house. It hurt so much, I could barely stand it. Was I going to drop dead at any moment?

I felt around in the dark until I found the kitchen light and flipped it on. I stumbled over to the sink, turned the faucet on, and submerged my arm underneath the cold water. It helped…a little.

I don't know how long I stood there, gasping for air, letting the water drench the skin on my arm as I waited for the pain to subside, but I was guessing it was quite a while. Finally, the fiery pain dwindled down, but it left in its place a few olive-green lines that traced across my veins on the lower half of my arm.

I touched the lines with my finger, pulling a face. I sure hoped it wasn't permanent.

I put my locket on and headed for the front door, to go look for a phone so I could call Aislin and tell her I was at the house. But as I went to shut the door behind me, I heard a soft *poof*.

I whirled around. A cloud of purple haze swirled through the room, and Alex, Laylen, and Aislin were standing in the center of it. They were all freaked out, eyes wide, mouths agape. Alex was the first to come running up to me, his bright green eyes wide with panic.

"Are you—are you okay?" he asked, rushing for me. He opened his arms, as if to hug me, but then stopped and pulled back.

I didn't take it personally. It was a good thing; we had been too touchy-feely already. But my insides tightened with the desire for his arms to be wrapped around me. I wanted him to hug me so badly I could barely stand it.

"I'm fine." My voice shook, giving away what I was feeling.

His eyes were all over me. "What did she do to you?"

I held out my arm, showing him the olive-green lines tracing my veins. "Her plants attacked me and then she touched me....you know, you could have warned me about the plants."

He cursed under his breath and examined my arm over without actually touching my skin. His gaze was enough, though, to dust a murmur of sparks across my skin. To make them stop, I moved my hand away and took a step back.

87

"It's not permanent, is it?" I asked worriedly.

Alex bit at his bottom lip. "It is."

I shook my head. "Great. Now I'm always going to have a reminder of when your ex-girlfriend tried to kill me."

Something about what I said set something off between the four of us. I don't know who laughed first, but suddenly we were all laughing hysterically. Maybe it was because we were all tired, or maybe it was because the idea that Alex's ex-girlfriend would try to kill me sounded so ridiculous; yet it was true.

So we all stood there and had our little laughing moment, until the darkness settled over us again and we had to move on.

In the living room, we all gathered around the mapping ball, the star-shaped light in the center illuminating a purple glow across each of our faces as Alex and Aislin and I explained to Laylen what had been going on while he was gone.

"So what do we do now?" I choked. "Now that...Nicholas is gone."

After I had gone to get the mapping ball out of its hiding place, I had asked Alex what exactly happened to Nicholas—he didn't just leave him on the side of the road, did he? Alex told me no, and that when one of the fey die, the fey themselves take care of them.

I wondered if fey had funerals. I wondered how they would mourn Nicholas. Did fey shed tears over death? Would they gather and tell stories of Nicholas?

"We need to make a plan," Aislin said, twirling her hair around her finger as she thought.

Alex gave her a *duh* look. "Thanks for clarifying the obvious, Aislin."

Aislin fired a glare at him. "Don't be rude."

"We need to go to the City of Crystal." I picked up the mapping ball from off the coffee table and turned it around in my hands. "So I can get inside this thing."

"You don't even know how to use it," Alex said. "Nicholas never explained it to you."

"I know." I gave Alex the same *duh* look he shot at Aislin. "But I do know I need to get the power from that big crystal ball inside the City of Crystal. I just need to figure out how to bring the power back."

"Gemma, you need to know exactly what you're doing before you even try to go to the City of Crystal," Alex told me, leaning over the coffee table, his eyes stressing the danger. "It's quite the risk sneaking in there when you aren't sure how to get the power." He reached over and took the mapping ball from me, with his thinking face on.

"Maybe there's another Foreseer we can ask," Aislin suggested.

If only it were that easy. Involving another Foreseer would mean involving another person in what was going on, which was extremely risky. Besides, I was beginning to question what side the Foreseers played on. I mean, look at my father.

"Maybe you could ask your father," Laylen said, twisting at his lip ring. "I mean, you've been there once, so why can't you go there again?"

Alex opened his mouth to argue, but then he looked at me. "Could you go back there? Do you know how?"

I considered this. When I had gone there, it was totally by accident. I mean, I didn't even know exactly what or where the place was.

"I don't know...." I chewed on my fingernails. "I'm not sure what my father would even do if I was able to get back to wherever he was. He wouldn't tell me hardly anything the last time I was there."

"Well, you'll just have to make him." Alex looked me straight in the eye. "Tell him you can't fix his mistakes, unless he tells you how and what they are."

I was still hesitant. "I think I need to talk to my mom. I mean, she might know something about all this." I glanced at the seashell clock hanging on the tan wall. Wow. It was late. I gave Aislin a funny look. "Shouldn't my mom be here by now?"

Aislin twisted her golden-blonde hair around her finger, looking on edge. "I don't know...maybe she had to go somewhere else besides the store."

I narrowed my eyes at her. "Nothing's open this late."

Alex and Laylen gave Aislin a quizzical glance. I'm glad I wasn't the only one noticing her weird behavior.

"What exactly did she say on the phone?" Alex asked.

Aislin quickly shook her head. "I don't know...I don't remember."

"Aislin," Alex warned. "What did she say?"

"I don't want to tell you!" Aislin cried, throwing her head down into her hands. "You two will just go and try to save her, and I can't take any more of it!"

"Any more of what?" Alex asked, his voice softening a little.

"You risking your life all the time." She raised her head and tears were dripping down her cheeks. "Dad's crazy, mom left, and you're all I have left."

"Aislin," Alex's voice was cautious. "I understand where you're coming from, but this is what I—we do. We're Keepers. We risk our lives and that's how things are."

I swallowed hard. I never knew their mom had run off, leaving them with a madman for a father.

"Well, you can tell me," I said to Aislin. "I'll go get her by myself."

"He won't let you." Her voice cracked.

"Yeah, he will," I assured. "Wherever she is, I'll go by myself."

Alex opened his mouth. "Like hell I'm going to—"

I covered his mouth with my hand, ignoring the heat of his lips on my palm. "If I foresee there, he doesn't have a choice."

"I'll go with her," Laylen chimed in, meeting my eyes. "You and I can go, and they can stay here."

I dropped my hand from Alex's mouth and he gave me a dirty look. Surprisingly, though, he said nothing.

Aislin burst into tears, sobbing so hysterically, I could barely hear her when she said, "She went to the Keepers' castle to try and kill my father."

Chapter 11

At first I thought I didn't hear her right. I mean, why would my mom do such an insane thing? It was crazy—she would have to be crazy...

Oh my God. "She's crazy," I whispered.

"She's not crazy," Alex said. "She just wants to protect you."

"And get herself killed in the process," I said. "To me, that seems like a pretty crazy thing to do."

"She's your mother, Gemma." Alex's voice was gentle. "It's the same thing she did when Stephan sent her to The Underworld—she was trying to protect you."

My eyes widened. "What if he sends her to The Underworld again?" *No, no, no, no, no.*

"Relax, Gemma," Alex reached over and placed his hand on mine. His touch brought an electric shock and he quickly pulled away. "We'll go get her."

"No *we* won't," I told him. "I will. Stephan doesn't need both of us showing up there. It would be like handing him the end of the world on a golden platter."

He let out a sharp laugh. "You actually think I'm going to let you go to the Keeper's castle by yourself?"

"No, I'm not letting you go with me," I said, mimicking his sharpness.

We burned fiery glares at each other.

"How do we even know Stephan's there?" Laylen interrupted.

"I don't know…On the phone all Jocelyn said was that she was going to the Keeper's castle to put a stop to Stephan," Aislin said. "I tried to talk her out of it, but she wouldn't listen and then she hung up on me."

"So we don't even know if Stephan's there?" I said. "She could just go to the castle and find it empty. I mean, the last time Alex and I were there—when we saved my mom from The Underworld, it looked like no one had been in the castle for a while."

Aislin twirled her hair around her finger so tightly it became tangled. "He might not be…but he might," she said, working to untangle her hair.

"Well, I need to go get her, regardless if Stephan's there or not." I was aiming for an indifferent tone, but I sounded more like I just drank fifteen cups of coffee. I stood up on my wobbly legs, preparing to head off to the doomful castle.

Alex stood up and stepped in front of me, a look of protest on his face as he opened his mouth to say something. But Aislin interrupted him.

"Just a second…I have an idea" She stood up and smoothed out the creases on her shorts. "There might be a way to find out exactly what's going on—if your mom's in trouble." She paused and we all stared at her in anticipation. "I can do a tracker on her."

"A tracker?" I asked. "What's that?"

She gave me a small smile. "It's a spell."

"Oh, okay...but, Aislin, why haven't we done this before?" I wondered. "On your father? So we know where he's at."

She swallowed hard. "I can't use magic on my father."

"Oh, okay," I said, figuring she meant it was too painful for her or something, which seemed weird, but okay. "You don't have to then."

"No, I mean I can't use magic on him. Literally." She let out a tired sigh. "When I was younger, he had me place a shield spell on him, so no witch could ever use magic on him....it was horrible. It took so much magic, my nose started to bleed and I passed out."

I felt sorry for her. "How old were you?"

"Twelve." She stared off, lost in her memories.

"That's why you passed out for those two days?" Alex asked, his jaw tightening with anger.

"I'm sorry, but he told me I had to." She was almost in tears. "And I was too young to understand that it probably was a bad thing."

"I'm not mad at you, it's just...." He popped his knuckles, his jaw still set tight. "He's such an asshole."

That was putting it mildly.

"Well, anyway." Aislin shook her head, shaking away the memory. "I can do a Tracker Spell, but I need a few things first."

I raised my eyebrows with intrigue. "What kind of things?"

She started listing off a bunch of stuff with eccentric names. Then she announced she was going to go search the internet for nearby places that sold witch supplies — stores similar to Adessa's. When I asked how far we would have to go, she told me not to worry, places like that were all over, and there was probably one right here in town.

And she was right.

I decided to go with her to the store, which was about ten miles out of town, right along the side of the highway. I figured if I went, I could hurry her up. The clock was ticking and driving me crazy. I needed to find out where my mom was and if she was okay. And not knowing was eating at my insides.

We were transporting to the witches' store since, a) it was a much quicker form of transportation and, b) we didn't have the car since the Tahoe was totaled.

"Please be careful," Alex told both of us as we prepared for our departure. "Just hurry up, get the stuff, and come back." He looked worried.

He had pulled me aside, while Aislin had been gathering her transporting stuff, to give me his pocket knife. What he was thinking was going to happen, was beyond me. We would be gone for like ten minutes. But I guess considering the circumstances, it probably was best to have a weapon on me, even if I didn't necessarily know how to use it very well.

Aislin chanted her magic words under her breath as she dipped the red crystal into the flame of the black candle. The smoke tinted red as she continued to repeat, *"Per is calx EGO lux lucis via,"* until the smoke swept us away.

It was a creepy place; that was for sure. It felt like I had stepped into a scary movie, where the car breaks down on the side of the road, and the only option I have is to go into the one and only rundown building. And when I go in, no one ever sees me again.

And of course it had to be late at night, with the darkness engulfing us. Thankfully there were a few lampposts, and the house's porch lights shined bright, making it grey instead of a pitch black.

"Are you sure this is the place?" I asked Aislin. The old house's wood siding was rotting, and the porch looked like it was going to cave in on the next person who dared step foot on it.

Aislin glanced around and then pointed at the numbers 44 on the front of the house. "Yeah, that's the number it had on the address on the website."

I looked at her solemnly. "This place has its own website?"

She nodded as she picked up her candle and crystal and tucked them into the pocket of her shorts. Then she started across the gravel parking lot, which, surprise, surprise, was vacant: there wasn't a single car. I followed after her, the gravel crunching under my DCs, my nerves coming unhinged with every step.

We trotted up the stairs and stepped onto the porch, which creaked loudly beneath our weight. Aislin raised her hand toward the doorknob, but hesitated.

"Do we just go in?" She glanced over her shoulder at me. "Or should we knock?"

I shrugged. "I don't know…Probably knock, I guess."

She knocked, and the screen door fell off its hinges. We scattered to the side as it crashed down on the porch.

Aislin's eyes went wide as she stared down at the fallen door. "*Shit.*"

I gave her a shocked look, because I had never heard her say that before.

"Sorry," she apologized, like I cared. "But I don't think that's a good start."

I shook my head. "I know…Are you sure there weren't any other witch supplies stores nearby that maybe aren't so….ominous?"

Aislin glanced at the broken door and then back at me. "Maybe it might be a good idea to go somewhere else. I mean, it doesn't even look like someone is here."

I nodded and we started down the stairs.

"There was a place I think in the next town over." She pointed to our left. "It's not much farther."

"Can I help you?"

The voice startled us, but not as much as the fact that she seemed to come out of nowhere. A woman stood at the bottom of the steps, her black hair blended into the night, along with her black dress, and her dark eyes weighed heavily on us.

"Umm…" Aislin shot me an 'oh-crap' look and then stuttered to the woman, "We were just…um…Is this Medea's Herbal Supply Shop?"

The woman's gaze bore into us as she assessed us over. "It is."

Aislin forced a smile. "Well, are you open?"

I was kind of hoping the woman would say no. Yes, I knew we needed to hurry — we needed to figure out where my mom was. But this woman brought a sense of discomfort that sent my stomach rolling and my feet wanting to bolt.

"I am open," she said, and my hope shattered to the ground. She ambled up the steps, the porch rocking with her movement. "I see you knocked my door down."

My heart hammered in my chest. "Yeah, sorry about that."

She gave me a glance over, and walked inside, motioning us to follower her.

Aislin and I exchanged a look like: should we run?

"Are you coming," the woman snapped impatiently.

Aislin sighed and we stepped inside.

The first thing I noticed was that the place stank, like garbage mixed with wet dog and old shoes. It was horrid. But I didn't dare plug my nose.

The walls were filthy, the wallpaper peeling away. The floor was made of the same rotting wood as the outside of the house and there were a few holes in the ceiling. A few shelves lined the walls, like at Adessa's. However, the objects that covered the shelves had a darker, more evil way about them.

"What exactly are you looking for?" The woman's eyes were cold.

Aislin rattled off a list of stuff and the woman looked even more annoyed by our presence. But she said she had everything and started digging around in boxes, collecting everything.

"So are you Medea?" Aislin asked, pointing up to a rusted sign on the wall that read: Medea's Herbal Supply Shop.

"I am," she—Medea said in an icy voice. She placed a few baggies onto the counter, each one filled with a different colored herb.

Aislin wandered around, tracing her fingers along the shelves, until she came across a thick book. She picked it up and looked at the cover. Then, giving a quick glance at Medea, stuffed it into her purse.

Hold on. Did Aislin just shoplift?

100

Medea was still taking out baggies and setting them on the counter. As she moved her hand out of the box, the sleeve of her black dressed rose up a little, giving me a glimpse of her wrist.

My heart stopped.

Tattooing her skin…a black triangle outlining a red symbol.

The Mark of Malefiscus.

As if she sensed me watching her, Medea glanced up. I averted my eyes to a tiny statue of a man with one eye. But I could feel her gaze boring into me, like a hawk watching its prey from the sky, about to swipe down and strike.

Oh, my God. Oh, my God. I needed to get Aislin's attention. Trying to act as casual as possible, I went over and stood beside Aislin, who was standing in the corner examining a small golden box with a flame decorating the lid.

"We have to go," I whispered. "Right now."

She gave me a confused look as she picked up the flame box.

I pointed at my wrist. *She has the Mark of Malefiscus on her wrist*, I mouthed.

What, Aislin mouthed back.

The Mark of Malefiscus, I mouthed, giving a discrete nod at Medea. *On her wrist.*

Panic rose on her face. "What do we do?" she whispered.

"Get the heck out of here," I whispered back, putting a hand on her arm. Then I shut my eyes to Foresee us out of there...but nothing. It wasn't working. There had to be *Praesidium* somewhere. Figures a witch store would have something like that. "My power's not working," I whispered to Aislin.

"Okay..." Aislin said with determination. "Follow my lead."

"What?"

But she was already walking away.

"Oh, shoot." She stomped her foot on the floor dramatically. "I forgot to bring money to pay for this."

I frowned at her. This was her plan. I mean, her purse was on her shoulder for crying out loud.

Medea gave her the most irritated look ever. "So you have no money."

"Not on me." Aislin walked for the door and I followed, trying not to rush. "But I can go back to my house really quick and come back...you could hold these for me." She pointed at the bags of herbs.

Medea's eyes grew darker as she tossed the bags of herbs back into the box.

"Well, okay, then," Aislin said, her nervousness starting to show. "We'll be back with some money."

And then we were hauling for the front door, like a couple of marathon speed walkers'. To my shock, Medea did nothing. She just stood there by the counter, watching us bolt.

102

But I wasn't complaining.

We reached the door and Aislin yanked it open. Strangely, the screen door was on its hinges. Aislin went to push it open, but it wouldn't budge.

"What the—"The main door swung shut and we jumped out of its way, both of us tumbling onto the floor.

"You two are not going anywhere," Medea roared.

Aislin and I scrambled to our feet, only to find the room empty.

"Where'd she go?" I asked, glancing around frantically.

Aislin was yanking on the door. "I don't know...Come on you stupid thing...open."

I grabbed her arm. "Come on. There's got to be another way out."

We ran across the room, our frantic footsteps vibrating the rickety floor.

"Going somewhere?" Medea's voice came up behind us.

I spun around, tripping over my own feet, and fell to the ground again. I jumped up, shaking off my soon-to-be-bruised knees. "Where is she?" The words rushed out of me.

Aislin glanced around desperately. "I don't know."

"Behind you," Medea's voice floated up over our shoulders.

We whirled around, only to find no one there again.

"She's taunting us," Aislin whispered. "She's using magic to play with our minds."

A black figure swished by us, knocking me into Aislin, and we both collapsed to the floor. We scurried to our feet again, only to be knocked right back down by the black figure.

I started to get to my feet, but Aislin caught me by the arm. "Just hold still."

We froze. The only sound I could hear was our breathing, loud and erratic—terrified.

"Where did she go?" I hissed through my teeth.

Aislin opened her mouth to say something, but then snapped it shut, because there she was—Medea, standing in front of us, the sleeves of her black dress rolled up so we could get a good look at the Mark of Malefiscus on her wrist.

"Do you know what this is?" Her dark eyes were locked on me.

I stayed silent.

"Do you know what this is!" she screamed, raising her wrist in front of her.

"Y-yes," I stammered.

"Then you are the one." She wasn't asking a question, but stating a fact. She knew I was the star—well, half of it anyway.

I glanced fearfully at Aislin. Her eyes were wide with terror and her hands were trembling. She was just as scared as I was.

104

Medea walked toward me, her heavy black boots making loud thuds with each step. "The question is: why are you here?"

No, I think the question was: why did she have the mark? "Why do you have that?" I pointed at her wrist.

She grazed her finger over the mark tattooing her wrist. "I was born with it."

Aislin and I traded a baffled look.

"What?" I said. "I thought only a descendent of Malefiscus could be born with the mark."

She smiled, showing us her decaying, yellow teeth. "The rise of his descendant has brought out all our marks. We are all followers of Stephan, our re-uniter of Malefiscus."

"All *our* marks?" What was going on?

Aislin shot me a look, warning me to keep my mouth shut.

"Oh, yes," Medea said. "Our marks. Witches, fey, and vampires, all waiting for Malefiscus, and his hundreds and hundreds of Death Walkers, to be free."

I guess that part had gotten lost in translation. My mother was under the impression that the marks would not come until after the portal opened and Malefiscus was freed. She also made it sound like a controlled thing, like the vampires, fey, and witches would be forced to follow him.

Guess she was wrong.

I slowly stood to my feet and Aislin did too. She still had the gold-flamed box grasped in her hand. "But if you all have the Mark of Malefiscus already, then why aren't you out there, hurting people?"

"All in good time," Medea said. "First, we need the Mark of Immortality."

Our jaws dropped.

"Oh, yes," Medea's face lit up with excitement. "Stephan is working to perfect the mark as we speak, and once he does, he'll put it on himself, therefore marking us all immortal."

I was struck speechless. Stephan was trying to mark himself with the Mark of Immortality. And if he did, every witch, fey, and vampire with the Mark of Malefiscus would become immortal too. So not a good thing.

Medea assessed me over, her gaze landing on my eyes. "I need to take you to him."

"No, you don't," I told her, taking a step back as I slipped the knife out of my pocket and flipped open the blade. "And I'm not going anywhere."

She smiled, rising to the challenge. "We'll see."

"No we won't!" Aislin screamed and threw the golden box at Medea.

It hit the floor in front of her feet and the lid flew off. Medea's dark eyes widened. There was a deafening roar and then she burst into flames.

"Run!" Aislin shouted, urging me to move.

And I did.

But Aislin didn't follow. I stopped as she ran over to the counter and grabbed the box Medea had put the bags of herbs into.

She skittered around the flames. "Go! Go!"

I sprinted past the burning Medea, with Aislin following at my heels. But when I tried to open the door, it was still locked.

"What do we do?" I cried over the crackle of the flames as I tugged on the door. "And why doesn't this place have any freaking windows."

The room was rapidly filling with smoke and the bright flames burned away at the floors and walls. Medea stood in the center of the fire, screaming at the top of her lungs, her hands thrown in the air.

Aislin ducked down to the floor. "Follow me."

We crawled through the thick smoke, heading to who knew where. I couldn't see a thing. Smoke filled my lungs and stung at my eyes. Finally, Aislin stopped crawling and pulled out her crystal and candle

"You're doing that here?" I asked, horrified, as I glanced back at the flames crackling toward us.

She didn't answer, fumbling with her lighter until she lit the wick of the black candle. Her hand trembled as she dipped the red crystal into the flame. *"Per is calx EGO lux lucis via."*

The heat of the fire melted at my shoes.

"Per is calx EGO lux lucis via."

My body was burning up.

107

"Per is calx EGO lux lucis via!"
I was flying, falling, suffocating.

Chapter 12

I landed in the living room of the beach house and tripped into the coffee table, knocking Aislin down with me. We both crashed onto the floor. The herb box Aislin had taken from Medea's flew out of her hands, sending baggies of herbs all over the place.

Five seconds later, Laylen and Alex were running into the room. They were both struck speechless by the sight of us, lying on the floor, ash coating our skin and clothes.

Alex finally found his voice. "What—what happened?" He rubbed my arm with his finger, wiping away some ash. "Is this ash?"

"Yeah." I coughed. "Well, it kind of turned out the store owner was this crazy witch with the Mark of Malefiscus."

Alex looked shocked. "Why do you have ash on you?"

"We burned her up." Aislin stood up and swept the ash off her clothes, while Laylen brushed some out of her hair.

Alex blinked at her. "You burned the witch up?"

"It's a long story." I started to get to my feet, but Alex took my hand and pulled me up. My hand tingled and I quickly slipped it away from his. Why did he have to touch me like that? It was torturous.

Alex flexed his hand. "So what were you saying about the witch being crazy?"

"And that she had the Mark of Malefiscus," I reminded him, sinking down on one of the sofas.

Alex sank down on the sofa beside me. "I thought you were kidding about that part?"

I shook my head and started to explain. While I did, Aislin went back into the bedroom to do the Tracker Spell, which would hopefully tell me what was going on with my mom, and if I was going to have to go on a rescue mission to save her.

"So there are others with the mark?" Alex asked after I finished.

"From what it sounded like, yeah, there are." I nodded. "And they're all just waiting around for Malefiscus to rise again or whatever."

Laylen bit at his lip ring. "And they all might become immortal—Stephan might become immortal?"

"If he can figure out how to make the mark," I explained, wiping some ash off the ugly olive-green lines on my arm. "But it sounds like he hasn't yet."

"We need to hurry then." Alex ran his fingers through his hair. "We need to figure out how to get you into that mapping ball to fix the vision."

Man, I could feel the pressure. "I know."

A small wall clock ticked in the background as we all took in the severity of the situation. We needed to save the world, by using the mapping ball, yet we didn't know how to use the mapping ball.

"But what if I change the vision back to whatever it was, and Stephan still lives?" I said, thinking out loud. "I mean I know Malefiscus won't be freed, along with a bunch of Death Walkers, but if there are already people with the Mark of Malefiscus, couldn't they still get together with Stephan and do some damage?"

Alex and Laylen both stared at me with stunned expressions. Apparently, neither of them had been considering this.

Before we could go on discussing the possibility, Aislin came barreling into the room, breathless and flushed. "I found your mom," she panted. "She's at the castle."

I think part of me was holding onto the hope that maybe my mom hadn't gone there; that she had started to, but then decided against it when she realized it was probably a suicide mission.

"It's bad too," Aislin said. "She's locked up in a room upstairs, and there are Death Walkers there, which means Stephan's probably there."

"Of course, he is." I sighed miserably. There was a time when Alex and I had both agreed nothing was ever easy. And it always seemed to be the case, at least in this world.

111

"Are you ready to go?" I asked Laylen. "Or, if you don't want to anymore, I can go by myself...I'll understand."

"Gemma," Laylen said, all serious and intense. "Of course, I'm going to go."

"Thank you." I almost gave him a hug, but decided against it, figuring it would be weird with an audience.

"But you should change into some pants first." Laylen pointed at the Levi shorts I was wearing. "It's freezing up there at night."

"Okay, give me a second." I started for the hall.

"I still think I should go," Alex said abruptly. "I don't see why I have to stay here."

I narrowed my eyes at him, not wanting to go down this road again. "We already went over this. It's not wise for both of us to go because Stephan needs both of us in order to open the portal."

He walked up to me and stood way too close for it to be in the safe-from-feelings boundary. "Then I should go and you should stay here."

"We already talked about this too." I inched myself back, smacking my elbow onto the wall. I rubbed my elbow. "Ow...You have a sister you would be leaving behind. I don't."

Intensity burned in his bright green eyes. "You're leaving me behind."

I didn't even know how to respond to that—I was too flustered and feeling things I knew I shouldn't be feeling—

so I turned away and headed off to my bedroom. Alex said something else, but when I shut the door it blocked out his words. And for a second, it blocked out all of the danger I was about to face. If only it were that easy. If only I could shut the door, lock myself in the room, and make my problems stay on the other side.

But like I said, nothing is ever easy.

I pulled on a pair of jeans, changed my shirt, and rinsed the ashes off my skin. Then I flopped down on the bed, trying to mentally prepare myself for what I was about to do. But I was sure that was impossible. I was so terrified, and deep down I wanted to run out of the room and tell Alex I changed my mind and he could go. But this was not his problem—it was mine.

Someone knocked at the door.

"Come in," I called out, figuring it was Laylen ready to get the show on the road.

But it wasn't Laylen. It was someone who I probably shouldn't be alone in a room with.

"You about ready?" Alex walked in and shut the door behind him.

I sat up and frowned at him. "I'm not taking you with me. You need to stay here with your sister." I tensed up under his gaze. "I never realized your mom left."

Still not speaking, he sat down on the bed, making me even tenser. Well, that and the fact that he was holding the Sword of Immortality.

113

"What are you doing?" I asked. "I mean in here...with me?"

He stared at the floor, his eyebrows dipping down. "My mom left when I was about five," he said suddenly and looked up and met my eyes. "At least, I think she left...I have to wonder now, after everything my father has done, if maybe he had something to do with it."

There was so much agony burdening his expression that I wanted to lie and tell him that that probably wasn't the case. But he would know it was a lie, and it would make things worse. I think in reality, we both knew Stephan probably had something to do with his mom disappearing.

"There's this rock at the back of the castle that hides a secret entryway to the basement," he said, still looking back at the floor. "Laylen should be able to lift the rock up so you guys can get in...no one knows it's there but me." He looked up and handed me the Sword of Immortality.

The jagged, silver blade glinted deathly in the light and the handle was cold against my skin. "What—why are you giving me this?"

"Because you might need it." He shut his eyes tight, as if he was in pain. "I want you to be able to protect yourself."

My heart thumped in my chest. "Thanks."

He paused and fear filled his eyes, which freaked me out even more because Alex rarely showed fear, especially such a powerful kind of fear.

114

"Can you promise me something?" He sounded breathless.

The word left my lips under no control of my own. "Anything."

It surprised both of us and seizing my rare moment of cooperativeness, he quickly said, "Promise me if anything happens at all—if anything even remotely bad looks like it will happen—you'll come right back."

I swallowed hard. "Alex, I can't—"

He placed his hand across my mouth. "I know you feel like you need to save her—and I completely understand that. But you also need to understand that you might be the one person who can save the world. So if it all comes down to it, you're going to have to save yourself."

I was breathing loudly, so loud the sound filled up the room.

He moved his hand away and suddenly he was panicking, his foot tapping madly against the floor. "I should be going with you."

"No, you shouldn't." I shook my head. "Aislin needs you. I—I didn't realize that about your mother." I stared down at my feet. "No one should be alone in the world." I swallowed the lump in my throat. "It hurts…a lot."

It was quiet for a moment as my thoughts drifted back to my old life filled with loneliness. As dangerous as my new life was, I don't think I would trade it back. I never wanted to go back to that.

"You need to let me start doing things on my own— let me make my own decisions." I met his eyes. "No one ever has."

He nodded. "I know I do."

Silence enclosed around us again.

"Gemma," Alex whispered, and I knew what the softness of his voice meant.

I should have stopped him—I know I should have— but I found that my lips were incapable of forming a refusal. So I let him lean in. I let him brush his lips against mine. I let him kiss me.

I waited until my skin started to heat, and then I pulled away. He nodded, as if he understood. Then we got up, and left the room as if nothing happened.

Laylen was a little freaked when he saw me holding the Sword of Immortality. And that was okay—I was a little freaked out by it too. I could just see myself doing something stupid, like tripping and accidently stabbing him with it.

It made me nervous.

I stood in the living room, one hand holding Laylen's hand and my other gripping the sword. My pulse pounded as I tried not to panic at the huge responsibility I had put on myself.

"Are you ready?" I asked, tilting my head up at the six-foot-four vampire.

"Are you ready?" he replied, his voice pressing me to make sure.

I nodded and shut my eyes. "I am…let's go…"

"Wait. Wait."

My eyes shot open as Aislin came running into the room. She tripped over a small maroon rug and shot it a dirty look as she stopped in front of me. "I have something for you."

I furrowed my eyebrows. "You have something for me?"

"Yeah," she said with an excited sparkle in her green eyes. "It's to help you see in the dark."

I thought she was going to hand me a flashlight or something, which didn't seem like such good idea. It would be like saying: 'Hey, we're right here, come and get us.' But instead she whispered, *"Iuvo vos animadverto,"* as she raised her hand and blew something in my face.

Instinctively, I dropped the sword and pressed my hands to my eyes. "Oh my God! What was that?"

"Oh, sorry," Aislin apologized. "I was just so excited because I figured out how to do it, but I guess I should have warned you."

I rubbed my eyes. "Thanks, but a warning would have been kind of nice."

"Jesus Christ, Aislin," Alex said sharply. "What were you thinking?"

"I was thinking I was giving her night vision," Aislin retorted.

117

I dropped my hands and blinked a few times. Every-thing looked normal. "Night vision?"

She smiled, looking a bit like her old cheerful self again—something I hadn't seen in a few days. "Yep, night vision. So you don't have to stumble around in the dark basically blind."

"What about Laylen?" I asked. "Can you blow your little dusty stuff in his eyes?"

"No need to." She looked at Laylen in a way I had never seen her look at him before—with a look that I won-dered if I sometimes gave Alex. "He already has night vision."

Laylen gave her the same look back, but quickly blinked it away. "Well, we should go." He carefully picked up the sword and handed it to me. "Are you sure you're going to be okay with this thing?

I gave Laylen an uncertain look, but Alex said, "She'll be fine."

Laylen had his own sword tucked away in the pocket of his black jeans, one that wouldn't kill a Death Walker, but would temporarily immobilize it. It would, however, kill Stephan.

I took Laylen's hand again and took a deep breath. My heart raced insanely as I cast one last glance at Alex, and a thought crossed my mind. Would I ever see him again? I shook the thought from my head—I would not go into this with such thoughts—and shut my eyes.

I saw the lake, the forest, the castle...Then I was falling.

Chapter 13

I landed in classic Gemma style, tripping over my own feet and plummeting for the grassy ground. Laylen was still holding onto my hand, though, and pulled me back up before my face hit the ground.

"Thanks," I told him, breathless.

He gave me a small smile. "No problem."

Wait a minute. I could see his smile as if it were day time. Was it day time? I glanced up at sky. The full moon beamed down amongst the silver speckles of stars. No, it was not daytime. It just looked that way, thanks to Aislin and her awesomeness.

"Amazing," I muttered, touching the corner of my eye.

"Pretty cool, huh?" Laylen asked and I nodded.

I purposely had taken us into the forest because, from there, we could see the castle without being seen. That way we could get an idea of what was going on, before we actually went inside.

Laylen and I started through the tall trees, heading for the castle. The grey-stone tower poked out from the tips of the trees, like an arrow. Twigs and leaves crunched under our shoes and the air was chilly. For a while neither of us spoke, but then, suddenly, I had to know something.

"Why did you go to Stasha's?" I blurted out, and then quickly lowered my voice. "Why did you go with her to her house?"

He considered this for what seemed like an eternity. "I was standing outside of the...Red Dragon...debating whether I wanted to go in or not, when she showed up out of the blue. I think she hangs out there sometimes, but she didn't want to admit it, so she pretended to be wandering around the area. She asked me if I wanted to go back to her house." He paused. "I went with her because the only other option I had was going inside the Red Dragon."

A club where evil hung out...yeah, I could see a girl like Stasha hanging out there.

I tugged the sleeve of my thermal shirt down, trying to cover up the ugly permanent lines on my arms. "I'm glad you left with her then, even if she is sort of crazy."

He laughed and for a split second, some of his pain vanished from his eyes.

"You know, Aislin was freaked out the whole time you were gone," I told him, dodging around a bush. "She cried practically the entire time."

"Aislin always cries," Laylen informed me, karate-chopping a low branch that was in his way. "She's been that way basically forever."

"Yeah, but do you think...maybe....it would help if you forgave her for what happened between you two." I

121

had no idea why I was saying this, and I worried I might have crossed a line.

He didn't answer, staring straight ahead through the darkness. "Did you cry while I was gone?"

I blinked up at him confusedly. "What?"

He met my eyes and tension clasped the air. "Did you cry while I was gone?"

"Oh, yeah, I cried until my tears ran out," I joked, trying to break the tension.

He smiled and shook his head. "I knew you were secretly pining for me."

I laughed and he did too. Then he swung his arm around me and pulled me into him.

"I'll try to fix things between Aislin and me, but it has to be a mutual thing," he said in a low voice. "She has to want me back in her life too, vampire and all."

I nodded. "Yeah, I know. And I have this feeling she will."

"But honestly, I could be okay with this." He kissed the top of my head. "Just you and me."

Part of me agreed with him—I could stay like this way forever. Just me and Laylen, the first friend I ever had.

We walked the rest of the way in the quiet stillness that only night brings. It wasn't awkward or anything, just a comfortable silence; the kind of silence that only exists between two people who are comfortable with each other.

The bright lights inside the castle lit up the outside, warning us there were people inside.

Laylen guided us behind a large oak tree when we reached the edge of the forest. "Okay...we're probably just going to have to make a run for the back." He peered around the corner of the tree trunk. "I don't see anyone outside." His eyes searched for something. "And I think I see the rock Alex was talking about." He met my eyes. "Are you sure you're ready for this?"

I clutched the Sword of Immortality in my trembling hand. "As ready as I'll ever be."

"Alright, then." He was nervous, which made me even more nervous. He raised his eyebrows at me. "On the count of three?" he asked and I nodded, crossing my fingers I didn't eat dirt during the sprint. "One...two...three."

We took off, charging through the night toward the ominous castle, our feet thudding in unison. I tripped over a rock, but caught myself and didn't endure anymore stumbles the rest of the way. The rock was gigantic—the size of a car at least—and it took Laylen quite some effort to scoot it forward. Beneath it was a small hole burrowed into the ground. Even with my night vision, I couldn't see the bottom. Laylen jumped into the hole first, since neither of us could tell how far of a drop it was, and Laylen was skilled in the art of enduring high falls.

"Alright, go ahead and jump," he called up once he reached the bottom.

123

Figuring it must not be too far of a drop, I sat down on the ground, slid my legs into the hole, and without any hesitation I jumped. I was wrong, though. It was a far jump. At least a few stories high. *At least.* But Laylen was there, in the darkness, breaking my fall as he caught me in his arms.

"Holy, crap," I breathed into his chest as I clasped tightly to his neck. "I didn't think it would be that far."

"I thought it would be easier if you didn't know," he replied, letting me go so I could stand.

He was right—it was easier.

It was the thickest darkness down here. "Can you see?" I whispered.

"Barely." Laylen took my hand. "This way," he said, guiding me with him as he walked through the blackness.

I'm not really afraid of the dark or anything, but this was scaring me to death. I mean, I didn't know this place, only that Stephan probably was around somewhere. And what if he was out there in the darkness, watching us as we wandered around blindly. What if we couldn't see him, but he could see us and he was just waiting for the perfect moment to—

"Gemma, take some deep breaths and try to relax." Laylen squeezed my hand. "Your heart's beating so loud I can hear it."

"Sorry." I took a deep breath, but I knew it wouldn't relax me. "It's just creepy, you know? I mean, I can't see a thing."

"I can see a little," he tried to reassure me. "We're in an empty tunnel. There's nothing here to worry about."

Worry about yet. I scooted in closer to him.

The tunnel seemed to last forever. And just when I thought I couldn't take it anymore, that the pitch black was never going to leave us, I could suddenly see again. But what I saw made me want to shrink back into the dark tunnel again. It made me want to run.

Laylen and I were standing in a torture chamber.

And we were not alone.

Chapter 14

"What is this place?" I whispered, staring at the pale figure, strapped to a rack in the center of the room.

Laylen shook his head. 'I have no idea…I've never been down here before."

"Should we…" I gestured at the person bound to the rack. "Should we free them?"

Laylen gave me a skeptical look and then slowly made his way over. I followed at his heels, trying to figure out if the person was alive or dead. Honestly, they looked dead, their eyes sealed shut, their body unmoving, their lips silent as a grave.

Even when we stood above them—or should I say her—she still showed no signs of life.

"Is she…is she alive?" I said to Laylen.

Laylen leaned over her. "Yeah, I can hear her heart beating."

"Should we…" I reached for one of the ropes around her wrist. "Should I untie her?"

Laylen nodded and reached for the other rope around her wrist. The rack wasn't stretching her limbs to their full capacity, but her pale skin was pulled rather tight. Her curly black hair ran off the sides of the rack, and so did the worn-out blue dress she was wearing. Laylen and I untied the ropes around her arms and her legs, but still she didn't move.

"Now what?" I wondered, reaching out as I considered giving her a soft shake.

But Laylen beat me to the punch, lightly shaking her shoulder. But still, she didn't show any signs of being alive.

"Maybe she's—" I started

The girl's eyes shot open. She took one look at us and leapt from the rack. She backed herself up against the stone wall like a skittish cat, her black curly hair a tangled mess around her face as she let out the loudest blood-curdling scream.

"Son of a..." Laylen jumped for her, grabbing her as gently as possible and covering her mouth with his hand. "We're not going to hurt you, but you have got to stop screaming."

The girl's bright yellow eyes were wild as she scanned the room, the rack, the stairway that twisted up to a door. Then, she caught sight of me and something in her expression changed. She calmed down.

Laylen slowly inched his hand away from her mouth, testing whether she was going to freak out and scream again. But she didn't. There was something about the sight of me that was calming her.

"It's you," she breathed loudly. "I can't believe it."

127

I glanced behind me, making sure there wasn't someone else she was looking at.

There was nothing there but the tunnel

"Yeah, it's me." I shot Laylen an is-she-crazy look and he shrugged.

"If I let you go, are you going to scream again?" Laylen asked her in a gentle tone.

The girl shook her head and he released her. Her bright yellow eyes stayed locked on me as she walked forward. Laylen, I guess getting nervous, stepped between us.

"You think you know her?" he asked, pointing at me.

She nodded. "She's the one he talks about all the time. The girl with the violet eyes—the star."

Well, holy crap. She did know who I was. "Who told you about me?" I asked, stepping up beside Laylen.

She glanced up apprehensively at the top of the spiral stairs. "The man with the scar," she whispered.

Stephan.

"Why did he tell you about her?" Laylen held out his arm in front of me, still trying to urge me to keep away from her.

"Because." She tilted her head, examining me over with her unnatural bright yellow eyes. "I'm the half faerie, half Keeper he needs for his plan."

She said it as if were nothing out of the ordinary, as if we should have known this bit of information already.

But it wasn't normal. At all. It was one of those things that made your jaw smack to the floor. At least that's what I thought until she tacked on, "And I'm his daughter."

Chapter 15

It was one of those moments where time freezes. No one moved. No one talked. No one breathed. As if we all had forgotten how to.

Laylen was the first one to find his voice. "I'm sorry, but I don't think you are...Aislin and Alex don't have a sister."

"Oh, I'm only their half-sister." She talked strange, as if using her voice was foreign to her. "And they don't know about me. My father keeps me hidden all the time. Down here." She gestured at the rack.

"Of course he does," Laylen said like something had just dawned on him.

"Why would he keep you hidden?" I asked.

"Keepers aren't supposed to mix like that with fey," Laylen explained to me, brushing his blue-tipped bangs away from his forehead. "There's something about the blood...too much mythical creature on one side and not enough on the other that creates an imbalance." He discretely nodded his head at the girl. "It makes things a little off."

How off? "What's your name?" I asked the girl.

She stuck out her hand awkwardly. "I'm Aleesa."

Laylen shook her hand politely. "Nice to meet you Aleesa."

I eyed over Aleesa and something didn't add up. "You don't really look like them. Alex and Aislin, I mean."

"Oh, I get my looks from my mother. She was fey," she said, like it explained everything.

It didn't.

"It's actually true," Laylen told me, finally lowering his arm from in front of me. "Many of the fey have bright yellow eyes and dark hair like hers. Nicholas was an exception."

Nicholas. It felt like someone was choking me. "So Stephan is your father," I croaked and Laylen gave me a funny look. "I mean, he created you for the plan...the end of the world plan."

She nodded. "Yes, I am the half-faerie, half-Keeper sacrifice he needs. I am what will bind the fey to him."

My eyes widened. "Sacrifice?"

"Yes," she said simply, her hands behind her back as she rocked forward on her toes.

The poor girl. She thought this was all alright.

I gazed around at the torture chamber, the rock walls, the cold cement floor, the rack. "How long have you been down here?"

She considered this, a look of perplexity twisting across her face. "I'm not sure. Forever, I think."

131

I shuddered. "Well, what about your mom? Where's she?"

"Oh, she's gone," she said with a shrug. "She left me."

I had no idea what to do with this. Obviously, we couldn't just leave her down here to be tortured by her own father. But she also made me kind of edgy because she seemed a little off her rocker.

"Laylen can I talk to you for just a second?" I backed away toward the tunnel, motioning him to follow me.

"What's up?" Laylen asked when we reached the edge of the tunnel.

"What are we going to do with her?" I said in a low voice.

He glanced over his shoulder at Aleesa, who was fiddling with a hole in the hem of her worn-out blue dress. "I guess take her with us."

His answer didn't really surprise me. That was the kind of guy Laylen was. "But is she...I don't know..." I tucked a piece of my long brown hair behind my ear. "She seems a little off. What if she flips out on us or something?"

His eyes filled with anguish. "I could flip out on you and yet you're still with me."

"Yeah, but you're...you. I trust you more than I trust anyone."

"Maybe you shouldn't."

I sighed. "We'll take her with us, then. But just keep an eye on her." I started for Aleesa, but stopped. "And I'll always trust you, Laylen. I'll trust you forever."

Getting Aleesa to leave with us proved to be a difficult task. First off, she kept saying over and over and over again that she wasn't allowed to go anywhere. But after some persuading, she finally agreed. That just left the task of trying to keep her quiet while we snuck upstairs to get my mom. I was worried she might snap and start screaming again or something. This was a concern of Laylen's too, and I suggested that maybe we should leave her here and pick her up on our way out. But after some deliberation, we decided we should take her just in case we had to make an emergency exit.

We crept up the spiral staircase, Laylen in front of me, Aleesa trailing along behind me. My palm sweated profusely against the handle of the Sword of Immortality, and suddenly, I started to panic about having it in my hand. Why did Alex give me the sword? I wasn't a Keeper. I hated to think it—considering who the leader of the Keepers was—but being a Keeper right now would have been real handy. I had seen Alex, Aislin, and even Laylen in motion; they were fast, strong, and graceful, and I really could have used these things at the moment.

"Okay," Laylen whispered when we reached the top of the stairs. "I have no idea what's on the other side of this door, so get ready."

I nodded, but my legs were shaking like a new born fawn learning how to walk. Laylen took a deep breath and creaked open the door, sticking the knife out in front of him like a master sword fighter, which he probably was.

He lowered the sword. "Coast is clear and it seems the secret entrance has led us to another secret entrance."

"What?" I asked as we cautiously stepped out into a hallway. "Why is this a secret entrance?"

Laylen brushed his fingers against the wall. "We're inside the wall."

I gaped at him. "How do you know?"

He winked at me. "Because I know all."

I shook my head as we started down the hall, making sure to glance behind me every few steps to check if Aleesa was still following.

She hummed quietly as she walked, glancing up at the ceiling and over at the walls, which were decorated with child-like art. I traced my fingers on the pictures, getting a sense of familiarity. Why did I know this?

Then it all came rushing back to me.

Alex and I as children, running up and down the hall, drawing on the walls, laughing, playing. I could almost hear the giggles still haunting the hallway.

"You okay?" Laylen's voice pulled me back.

134

I realized I had stopped. "Yeah," I shook my head. "Sorry."

We crept down the rest of the hall, until we reached a door.

"What's on the other side?" I whispered.

"A spare bedroom," Laylen said, clutching onto the doorknob. "I wonder if it's emp—"

A muffled cry came from the other side of the door.

"Oh my God, it's my mom." I reached for the doorknob, but Laylen pushed my hand back.

"Just calm down," he said softly and squatted down. "Jocelyn," he whispered through the door. "Is that you?"

The crying stopped.

"Open the door," I hurried Laylen.

"Make sure to keep calm," he said, and then creaked open the door.

The room was empty except for my mom, chained to the wall, like a prisoner. She had just escaped from being one a few days ago and it tore at me heart to see her like this. She looked like she was sleeping, her head hung down, her shoulders slumped. There was a piece of ducttape over her mouth and I carefully pulled it off.

"Mom," I said. "Can you hear me?"

Her head wobbled as she looked up and blinked at me, tears streaming down her face. "Gemma," she croaked.

"It's okay, Mom," I said softly. "We're going to get you out of here."

135

She blinked again, still a little dazed. Then suddenly she was going crazy. "You have to go. You have to go now." She was tugging at the chains. "It's a trap. Gemma, go! GO!"

A canopy of gloom covered the room as a chill slithered into the air. I turned around, my heart pounding like a jack hammer as a thick fog crawled across the stone floor and swirled around my ankles. Cold crackled across the maroon walls and ceiling, coating them with icicles.

Do not panic, I told myself. To Laylen I said, "Can you get the chains off her?"

He nodded and grabbed the chains binding my mom's wrists to the walls. He bent them and flexed them, trying to get the heavy metal to snap. But the chains were thick and covered with the Death Walker's ice, and I could tell it was going to take him a moment.

I needed to prepare myself. I stood in the middle of the room, sword in hand, with no clue as to what I was going to do.

Aleesa let out a high-pitched scream, covered her ears, and backed into the corner of the room like a terrified little mouse.

Well, if they didn't know we were here before, they sure did now.

The footsteps came, like a marching army, one by one, marching right for us. I glanced back at Laylen, still struggling to get the chains undone.

136

"I'm hurrying, I'm hurrying," he said, bending at the metal links. "The damn things are thick and the ice is making it worse."

I blocked him out—I blocked everything out. Something was taking over my body. A power I had never felt before.

And suddenly I knew what to do.

I held the Sword of Immortality in front of me, steadied in the perfect position that I knew any sword master would appreciate. My heart-rate slowed, my nerves calmed, and as the first black-cloaked figure entered the room, I swung the sword, stabbing it straight into its heart. Its yellow eyes lit up as its corpse-like body dropped to the floor.

I didn't have time to prepare myself as another one walked into the room. I did this weird twirling thing that should have resulted with me landing on my face, but instead the sword jabbed into the Death Walker's heart. I swung the sword again and again, the tip sinking through each of their rotting chests. The bodies were piling up as I moved like a pro, swinging the sword gracefully, my feet moving harmoniously along with it.

But more and more came charging in and before I knew it, the room was filled with Death Walkers. They circled me, the yellow-glowing-eyed monsters, and my body temperature started to descend. I glanced down at my hands, but they hadn't turned blue yet.

And then Stephan walked in.

He was dressed head-to-toe in black, and he gazed at the Death Walkers' bodies piled all over the floor, looking both annoyed and impressed.

"Well, I see that you've changed since the last time I met you," he said unhappily.

He walked toward me, his boots cracking the ice covering the floors.

I stayed where I was, not stepping back, waiting until he was in sword's reach, and then took a swing at him. But he flicked the sword away as if my new inner strength was nothing but a minor glitch to him.

"You know, you are a very hard girl to track down," he said. "I send a faerie to find you, but he up and disappears. I try to find you myself, but I never can seem to find you. So, finally, I thought to myself, what can I do? How can I get ahold of my star?" He traced the scar grazing his left cheek, where his Mark of Malefiscus once existed, until his parents cut it off. "Then, an idea hit me. If I can't find you, why don't I have you find me?" He walked in a circle around me with his hands behind his back. "See, the thing is, Gemma, there's something you don't understand." He gave a dramatic pause. "I always win."

I dared a quick glance over my shoulder, relieved to find that Laylen had gotten the chains freed from around my mother's wrists. Now, if I could just get all three of us out...I glanced over at Aleesa, curled in the corner...all four of us.

"I wouldn't put so much trust in people, Gemma." Stephan's voice ripped me back to him. "You never know what secrets they could be hiding."

"And you would be the expert on that, wouldn't you?" I asked, looking him straight in the eye.

He smiled, but my confidence seemed to take him back a little. "I'm not the only one in this room who is an expert at lying." His gaze flickered behind me and I turned to find he was looking at my mother, sitting on the floor, her blue eyes saddened. "Should I tell her? Or would you like to, Jocelyn?"

I stared at my mom, waiting for her to explain what was going on. But she hung her head, refusing to look at me.

Laylen gave me an uneasy glance and I nodded my head Aleesa, signaling for him to get her and bring her closer.

"Ask her what's on her wrist," Stephan said. "Go ahead."

I think I already knew. "No...I—"

Laylen rolled up the sleeve of my mother's faded grey shirt and there it was. A triangle outlining a red symbol.

"No," I whispered, horrified. "How..."

"She's had it forever, you know. Sophia, Marco...Didn't you ever wonder how I got everyone to do what I asked? The only ones I didn't mark were the ones who couldn't be marked." He frowned disappointedly.

139

Was he referring to Laylen, Aislin, Alex, and me...and also Aleesa?

"Your mother's a fighter," Stephan continued. "She was always a fighter...it's her gift, you know—her Keeper's gift. She always made things difficult for me, which is part of the reason why I sent her to The Underworld. In fact, I couldn't even summon her to go—I had to threaten her with you." He let out a breath of frustration. "The Underworld has weakened her, though." An evil smile crept across his face. "It has tainted her, which makes things easier for me. Getting her to come here was as easy as a master whistling to call his dog." His dark-eyed gaze landed on my mother. "Makes her easier to control...All I had to do was tug at the leash a little."

Okay, this conversation was getting a little too metaphorical for me.

He turned his back to me and began rolling up the sleeves of his black button down shirt as if he was getting ready to fight me. A small part of me wanted to see how that fight would turn out, especially with my newfound badass fighting skills. But the other part of me knew what needed to be done.

With one swift dive, I slid across the icy floor, slipping between the two Death Walkers' legs and into my mom like a baseball player slides into home plate. I grabbed hold of Laylen's arm, and extended a hand out to Aleesa. She looked horrified but, thankfully, she took hold of it.

Stephan turned around and his face dropped.

"Get her!" he screamed at the Death Walkers, but it was too late.

We were already gone.

Chapter 16

I knew as soon as we landed in the living room that we need to get the heck out of the beach house. It was as if I had gained these awesome leadership skills.

"We have to go," I ordered, already on my feet, because that's how I landed (go figure).

Alex and Aislin were stunned into a silent state of shock at the sight of the extra passenger with us. But I didn't have time to explain to them who Aleesa was; that conversation was going to take some time.

I squatted down to eye level with my mom. "Mom, did you tell him where we were hiding?"

She was trembling. "I'm so sorry, Gemma. I wanted to tell you, but I couldn't."

"Okay, but I need to know if you told Stephan where we were hiding."

She didn't answer and, I think, it was because she couldn't.

So I made the call. "We need to leave now."

Alex was right in front of me when I stood up.

"Why do we need to leave?" He pointed at Aleesa, freaking out in the corner. "And who the hell is she?"

"She's just someone we found in the basement," I told him.

He raised an eyebrow at me. "So, then, why do we need to leave?"

I raised my mom's arm, rolled back her sleeve, and gave an exaggerated gesture towards her marked wrist. "Because of that."

His jaw nearly hit the floor. "What the…did he just do that to her?"

I shook my head. "But I'll explain everything later, okay? I think she told him where we were hiding."

His eyes widened and he called out, "Alright, everyone, we're leaving."

"Why?" Aislin looked so confused.

"Because we have to," was the only reason Alex gave her.

"Any suggestions on where we should go?" I asked, grabbing the glittering purple mapping ball off the coffee table.

"I'm running out of ideas," Alex said, dragging his fingers through his hair. "With all the moving around we've been doing."

Silence. Well, except for Aleesa's whines and my mother's sobbing.

"What if we went back to Afton?" I asked, practically choking on my own words.

143

"Gemma, Stephan knows where that is," Aislin said, like I was an idiot.

"Yeah, which means he's less likely to look for us there," I explained. "He would never think we would go to a place he knew about."

Alex mulled this over. "You know, that actually makes a lot of sense. I mean, Marco and Sophia abandoned it...and there was something about Afton that was supposed to preserve the energy of the star...so maybe going there will help," he gestured between himself and me, "our little fading problem."

I nodded. "So, to Afton it is."

"Look at you," Laylen joked with a smile. "First the badass ninja moves and now the awesome leadership skills."

Alex gave me a weird look. "Ninja moves?"

I waved him off. "I'll explain later...now what's the best way to get there?" I paused. "Aislin, how fast can you do a Tracker Spell?"

She tapped her finger on her lips. "Pretty quick if you need me to."

"Can you do it before we go and make sure Marco and Sophia aren't there?"

She nodded, already heading out of the room.

"How should we go there?" I asked Alex. "To Afton?"

"Either by transporting," Alex said, peering out the blinds. "Or with your power, seeing how we don't have a car anymore."

144

I glanced around at the five of us—plus Aislin in the bedroom—realizing how many people I was going to have to move if I opted for using my Foreseer power.

Alex continued to watch out the blinds until Aislin returned, while Laylen tried to calm Aleesa down. I think Alex was watching to make sure his father didn't show up, but really, I figured it would take him a while since Stephan didn't seem to have a quick way of traveling.

"They're not there, at the house," Aislin informed us when she entered the room. Something about her expression made me wonder where Marco and Sophia were—that maybe something bad happened to them.

I wasn't sure how I felt about that.

"How do you think we should get to Afton?" I asked Aislin.

"There's too many for me to transport at once," Aislin said, gathering her bag of herbs into the box. "But I could make two trips."

"No!" Alex and I yelled at the same time and she flinched.

"Sorry," Alex said. "But remember what happened the last time we did that?"

Aislin nodded, putting the lid on the box. "Yeah, I remember." She shuddered.

"It's okay...I can do it," I told him, hoping the extra adrenaline pumping through me at the moment would give me the extra boost I needed.

"Are you sure?" Alex asked, locking eyes with me.

I knew what he was doing. He was letting me make my own decisions, even though he might not like what I chose.

"I'm sure," I said with confidence.

I gathered everyone in a group as tightly as I could, and then I shut my eyes, picturing the high mountains, the red brick house I grew up in, centered in the middle of them. I tried not to cringe at the picture. But when I opened my eyes, I did cringe.

All six of us were huddled together, in the center of my old living room. I slowly stood up, a mixture of feelings pouring through me a hundred miles a minute. Everything...It was too much.

My eyes rolled into the back of my head and my body collapsed to the floor.

Chapter 17

The icy lake glistened before me, Alex stood beside me. My hand was in his, and I could feel his racing pulse. He was scared. I was scared.

Tears streamed down my cheeks, and Alex brushed them away with his finger.

"Don't cry." He leaned in, his lips a sliver of air away. "It will be alright."

"Will it?" I asked.

He kissed me like I was everything. "It will."

Tears dripped down my frostbitten cheeks. "How do you know?"

"Because I'll save you," he whispered. "I'll always save you, Gemma."

When I woke up, I was lying in my old bed. It freaked me out for a split second, like maybe I had dreamt the last few weeks and had finally woken up back in my lonely old Gemma life, friendless and with nothing.

But it couldn't have been a dream. It just couldn't.

I pinched myself just to make sure, and, yep, I was awake.

Everything looked exactly the same. The walls were still a boring tan and a single shelf sat in the corner that held my books and CDs. The only thing that was different was the six-foot-four vampire snoring away in my computer chair, his feet kicked up on the computer desk, his head tipped back in the most awkward position.

I found myself smiling at the picture. I crept out of bed and padded softly over to him. I didn't try to wake him right away. I just stood in front of him, taking in his pale skin, the silver lip ring looping his bottom lip, and the mark of immortality on his arm. God, he was beautiful. Although, he could snore like no other.

I lightly tapped him on the shoulder, figuring I would wake him up and see what was going on...and why he was snoring in my room?

He jumped, startled, and let out a loud snort.

"Sorry." I covered my mouth to stifle a laugh. "I didn't mean to scare you."

His bright blue eyes were huge and he pressed his hand to his heart. "You scared that crap out of me."

"Sorry," I apologized again. "But why are you sleeping at my computer desk?"

"I was on Gemma duty." He sat up and dropped his feet to the floor, his black boots hitting the carpet with a thud.

I raised my eyebrows questioningly. "Gemma duty?"

"Yeah, Gemma duty." Laylen fiddled with his lip ring. "You've been out for almost three days and we were getting a little worried about you...that maybe the *rush* was too much for you."

"What *rush*?" I asked, picking up a CD case from off the computer desk. I turned it over in my hands. Alkaline Trio—hadn't listened to them in a while.

"Yeah, the *rush*," Laylen said, swiveling in the chair. "It's what we call the rush of adrenaline you get when your Keeper's mark first appears."

My arms went limp, and the CD case fell from hands. "My Keeper's mark? I don't have a Keeper's mark."

He smiled, but it wasn't a happy kind of smile. "Yeah you do...on your shoulder blade."

I shook my head as I rushed over to the mirror and yanked down the upper part of my black t-shirt. "Holy..." Circling the center of my shoulder blade was a ring of fiery-gold flames. "Wait." I gave him a suspicious glance. "How did you guys find the mark on me?"

He gave me a sneaky smile. "How do you think?"

I picked up a pillow from off my bed and threw it at him.

He caught the pillow effortlessly. "I'm joking. We just checked the obvious places—the arms, the ankles, the shoulders. If we wouldn't have been able to find it, we would have waited for you to wake up."

I wondered who he meant when he said "we," but I didn't ask. I touched the mark on my shoulder. "God, I can't believe I'm a Keeper."

"You didn't think those awesome fighting moves came from nowhere, did you?" Laylen joked, cocking an eyebrow at me.

"So, you knew what was going on back at the castle?"

"I assumed as much."

I picked up the CD case and set it back on the desk. "So what's been going on for the last few days while I was out?"

"Not much," he said. "In fact, it's been pretty quiet."

I glanced over at the window, at the green grass lining the yard, kissed with the early morning's dew. That was one thing about the summers in Afton: they were very green. "What about my mom?" My voice was barely there. "How's she doing?"

He hesitated, fiddling with a loose string on the pillow he was still holding. "Everyone thought it would be best, including herself, to lock her up until we can figure out what to do with her. I mean, we don't want her sneaking off and doing something like what she just did."

"It wasn't her fault," I said quietly. "It's the mark's fault; she can't help it."

"I know it is." Laylen tossed the pillow aside. "But we have to be careful."

150

"Well, can't we try and figure out a way to remove the mark?" I asked "Maybe with magic, like what we were going to do with…Nicholas."

"Aislin's already on that," he explained. "She's been searching the internet like crazy for the last few days, but no luck yet. The problem is we don't know who to trust. After everything, she can't just go walking into a witch store and ask how to remove the Mark of Malefiscus." He stood up, went over to my shelf, and examined the row of CD's. "Aislin also went pretty spell crazy; she put like a ton of spells all over the house, trying to keep us protected."

I sat down on my bed as he skimmed my CD titles. "That was smart of her."

He nodded, sliding out a CD.

I sat in silence, feeling uncomfortable. Being in here, it was weird and it felt…Well, it felt wrong.

"What's up?"

I blinked up and found Laylen staring down at me, with a puzzled look on his face.

"You look like something's bothering you," he said, concerned.

"No…" I paused. "It's just that it's so weird to be in here again."

His eyebrows dipped down. "In your room?"

I nodded, eyeballing my old stuff. "It doesn't feel that way, though. Nothing about this room feels like me."

He gazed around my room, taking in the bareness. "Well, maybe that's because this room isn't you. I mean, all those years you spent here—were you ever really you?"

I shrugged. "I don't think I really know who I am yet."

"And that's okay." He wrapped his arm around me and pulled me in for a hug. "You'll figure out. Just give it time."

I sure hoped he was right.

He pulled me up from the bed and we headed out of the room to announce that I was indeed alright and hadn't died from an adrenaline overdose, which Laylen told me was actually a rare occurrence in the Keepers' world.

"So have you already explained to Aislin and Alex who Aleesa is?" I asked once we were out in the hall.

"I kind of had to," Laylen said as we trotted down the stairs.

"And how did they take it?"

"Pretty bad at first, but I think she's growing on them."

"And how's she doing?" I asked, thinking of her life stuck in the basement. I didn't know what was worse; being emotionally hollow for most of your life, or being locked away in a torture room, strapped to a rack.

"She's…okay." Laylen pointed back over his shoulder. "She's sleeping in the guest room right now….she sleeps a lot. And eats a lot. I don't think Stephan was feeding her that well."

152

I paused at the bottom of the stairs. "Why would he do that? Why would he lock her away and starve her…and torture her?"

"For a few reasons, probably," Laylen said. "One, being that he didn't want anyone to know about her, considering what she is. And I'm also guessing it probably has something to do with the fact that he purposely secluded me from the living, drained you of your emotions, and taught his son to emotionally shut off."

"What about Aislin?" I asked in a low voice, leaning in. "It doesn't seem like he's done anything to her."

He raised his eyebrows at me. "Hasn't he? I mean, she'll practically do whatever he says."

"Not anymore, though."

"No one does what he says anymore," Laylen pointed out.

"Yeah, I guess so," I said as we entered the living room.

Aislin was sitting cross-legged on the floor with a lap top resting on her lap, and Alex sat on the sofa, watching TV. Hmmm….what was wrong with this picture? Oh, yeah, it looked normal.

Upon closer look, I noticed Aislin was searching the web for mark removal spells, and Alex was sharpening a sword as he stared blankly at the TV. Yeah, that seemed more fitting.

"Oh, thank God." Aislin pressed her hand to her heart and let out a relieved sigh when she saw me. "I thought you weren't going to wake up."

"You guys always think that," I joked. "Yet I always do."

Aislin clicked the computer mouse. "Wow, you seem in a good mood."

I gave her a funny look. "Do I?"

"It's because of the lingering adrenaline from the *rush*." Alex turned around and gave me a lingering look that made my skin hum. "So you're a Keeper after all."

"I guess so," I said, trying not to squirm under his intense gaze. But, God, it was so intense, and suddenly I wanted to lean down, run my hands through his messily-in-an-intentional-kind-of-way hair, and press my lips to his.

Whoa.

"So," Laylen said, changing the subject. "What's our next move?"

He sat down on the floor beside Aislin and I took a seat in the chair behind them. Across from me Alex sat, still looking at me with way too much heat glowing in his bright green eyes. Was he trying to kill me or something?

"Has anyone talked to my mother?" I asked. "I mean, what happened? Or could she even tell you?"

"After we made the same Blood Promise with her as we did with Nicholas, then yeah, we got some information

154

out of her." Alex raised his hand, showing me a fresh cut on the palm of his hand.

"You didn't tie her to the garage ceiling and beat her up first, did you?" I asked, half joking, but half serious.

Alex let out an amused laugh and shook his head. "No, Gemma, I didn't beat your mom up."

"So what did she tell you?" I brushed my hair out of my face. "Did she say how she ended up at the Keeper's Castle?"

Alex's face grew grave. "*He* called her."

"But my mom doesn't have a phone?" I pointed out. At least I thought she didn't, since she just got out The Underworld a few days ago, and I'm pretty sure reception down there is nonexistent.

"No, he *called* her," Alex said, setting his sword on the table "As in he *summoned* her."

I leaned back and folded my arms. "Summoned?"

"Apparently, Stephan can summon people with the Mark of Malefiscus," Laylen said, looking over Aislin's shoulder as she typed something on the computer.

"How exactly does that work?" I asked.

Laylen glanced at Alex. "We have no idea, and neither does Jocelyn. All she said was that she suddenly felt compelled to go to the castle, so she did."

I tapped my foot anxiously. "How do we know he's not going to summon her right now?"

"We don't know," Alex said straightforwardly. "But we've got her locked up and we took away her Key of Malefiscus."

I frowned. "Key of Malefiscus. He has his own key now."

"He's had one all along," Alex said with this bitter/sarcastic tone. "Apparently, as Stephan marked each one of the Keepers' with the Mark of Malefiscus, he also gave them a key, so when he touches his scar, they can take the key, trace a door, and *Voila*—they're at the castle."

"What the..." I shook my head in astonishment. "So Nicholas had one of these too. And Marco and Sophia."

Aislin gasped when I mentioned Marco and Sophia's names. I gave her a funny look, but she avoided eye contact with me.

"Nicholas didn't have one, I don't think," Alex said. "Jocelyn said that Stephan gave them to the Keepers he marked."

"I still can't believe it...all this time...my mom...." I shook my head, thinking about before, when I knew nothing about her—when I thought she was dead—and I used to wonder what kind of a person she had been. And now I had her back, but it turned out she was marked with evil.

"Gemma." Alex voice was cautious. "I think you should go talk to your mom about this...there are some other things you need to know and I think you should hear them from her."

"Bad things?" I asked, even though I was sure they were.

He wavered momentarily. "Not necessary bad things, but things you need to know."

I nodded and got to my feet. "Where is she?"

He pointed over his shoulder at the stairs. "Up in Marco and Sophia's old room."

He gave me one more look that made me feel like I was some sort of Greek goddess shimmering in the sunlight, and then I headed off up the stairs to go chat about the dark side with my mom.

She looked miserable, lying on the floor, bound to the wall by chains. What I was wondering, though, was where all the stuff came from? The hooks in the wall that held the chains—the chains themselves. Had Marco and Sophia owned this stuff or had someone went out and bought them?

Her head was resting on a pillow, her brown hair a tangled mess. Her eyes were shut and she was breathing softly.

I shut the door behind me and her eyes shot open.

"Sorry, I didn't mean to wake you up," I said apologetically.

She sat up and I went over and sat cross-legged on the floor in front of her. We both stared at one another, not knowing where to start.

"I'm sorry, Gemma," she finally said with a guilty look on her face.

I traced a star pattern in the carpet with my finger. "It's okay. I understand you couldn't say anything about the mark to me." I paused. "But there's one thing I don't understand. How is it you're marked, yet you went to The Underworld to protect me? And how was it you could tell us all those things that day—about the ending of the world? Shouldn't the mark have stopped you?"

She shook her head. "There are always loopholes, Gemma."

"You keep saying that, but it doesn't make sense to me at all."

"I know. Some things are hard to understand and even harder to explain." She rested her head back against the wall. "Sometimes my mind gets all cloudy as if it doesn't belong to me, and I say words that aren't my own." She traced the cut of the Blood Promise on the palm of her hand. "It's not cloudy right now, but it won't last forever."

"The Blood Promise won't?" I asked.

She shook her head sadly. "I won't."

She was freaking me out. "What do you mean? You're not leaving me again, are you?"

She didn't answer right away, and when she did speak, she dodged around my question. "Remember how you told me that you saw the vision of Stephan forcing me into the lake?"

I nodded. "How could I forget?"

She smiled, but it was forced. "Well, you didn't understand the vision completely; there were things that happened that confused you."

"Like what?" I asked.

She let out a sigh. "Stephan didn't force me into the lake, like he—and you—thought. I went in there on my own....I chose to go to The Underworld on my own."

I was shaking my head. "No you didn't...I saw him force you to go in there."

She reached for my hand, the chains dragging across the floor. "No, you didn't. That's what it may have looked like, but that's not what happened." I was still shaking my head as she continued on, "I've always had this gift....kind of like super willpower, and for the longest time, even after Stephan marked me, it stayed with me—made me strong."

"How did he mark you?" I asked. "How did he mark everyone? Didn't anyone fight back?"

"That's hard to do when there are Death Walker's there," she explained, her blue eyes drifting off into empty space. "He picked us off one by one...And some didn't make it out alive...like Laylen's parents."

"I—I—But he told me his parents died in a car accident right after you were sent to The Underworld?"

"No, they died putting up a fight it when Stephan ambushed them."

I swallowed hard. "Does Laylen know this?"

159

She shook her head. "There is a lot of memory tampering that has gone on throughout the years, including with Laylen."

I remembered Laylen mentioning memory loss once, when he had been changed into a vampire, and he couldn't remember how.

"But why did you want to go to The Underworld?" I asked, fearing her answer. "Why would you ever *want* to go to a place like that? So full of death and torture?"

"Because I could feel Stephan gaining control over me," she whispered. "I was the hardest to gain control over. Even after he marked me, he still couldn't get me to do things, especially when it came to you. But he kept working and breaking me down and finally I felt it diminishing—my gift. I knew it wouldn't be long before I wouldn't have the say, and I just couldn't do it—I couldn't just stand around and watch them detach your soul and ruin your life."

"So you decided just to leave me then?" I was trying not to get angry, but it was hard. "Even though you knew they would still take away my soul?"

"I'm sorry." She tightened her grip on my hands, her bright blue irises pressing me to understand. "But even if I stayed, it would have happened."

So that was it. My mom had never sacrificed her life to try and save mine. She had sacrificed it so she wouldn't have to watch my life get ruined.

160

"So you wish I would have never went and saved you from The Underworld?" My anger was starting to show through my voice. "Do you wish I would have left you there?"

"*No*. I understand now that running away never solves anything. Everything still happened to you, and instead of trying to fight, I gave up. I will never give up again. We will figure out a way to fix this."

All of a sudden, I felt so alone, even with my mom in the room. "And how are we supposed to fix them? Do you know how to work a mapping ball?"

Her mouth curved to a frown. "Alex told me about that...So you saw your father?"

"Yeah...I saw him," I said.

"And did he tell you what he did?" she asked in a clipped tone. "Did he tell you how he ended the world?"

"Kind of...he said he made some mistakes and changed and recreated a vision so the world would end."

"Did he tell you why he did it?" The tone of her voice was piercing.

I shook my head slowly. "No, he never said why."

"Because he wanted this." She rolled back the sleeve of her shirt and held up her arm, showing me the Mark of Malefiscus on her wrist.

"No." I scooted away from her. "No, that's not true."

She took me by the shoulders and looked me straight in the eye. "Yes, he did. He wanted the mark...he wanted the mark"

"Why!?" I cried, tears dripping from my eyes.

She looked livid. "For power—he wanted to be powerful, just like Stephan."

I jumped to my feet, trembling with anger. "You're lying. He wouldn't be trying to fix it, if that was the case."

"Time changes peoples' minds, Gemma." She tried to get to her feet, but the weight of the chains dragged her back down. "And he's been locked up alone in the Room of Forbidden for so long, I'm sure he's had time to clear all the power hunger out of his head."

"No, you're lying!" I screamed. How could this be true? My father made this mess all because he had wanted to be powerful like Stephan, because he wanted the Mark of Malefiscus.

I turned around and stormed out of the room. My mother called my name, but I slammed the door, stomped down the hall, and burst into my room.

All this time, spent in here, wondering about my parents, only to find out that one wanted to be evil and one was marked with evil.

I snatched a brush from off my dresser and chucked it across the room. It made a loud thump as it dented the wall, and bits and pieces of tan paint and drywall crumbled to the floor.

"Good job, Gemma. Like that's going to help," I muttered to myself.

I slumped to the floor and rested my head against the door. What was I supposed to do? Try to get back to where my dad is—to this Room of Forbidden—and get some more details on how to fix his mistakes? I wasn't sure I wanted to do that. Not after what I had just been told.

"Ah! What am I going to do?"

Just as I said it, the sunlight hit my window and fluttered through my room. Something on my bed twinkled red. I slowly got to my feet, and my heart just about leapt out of my throat.

A miniature ruby-filled crystal ball glistened from the middle of my bed. I glanced around my room. Where did this come from? I inched my way over and picked up the tiny crystal ball. Underneath it was a piece of paper.

Go to the City of Crystal and get the Purple Flame.

Sincerely,

A friend

I flipped the paper over, but there was nothing on the back. Who left this? Who had been in my room? I went over to the window, pushed it open, and glanced down below. There was no one there on the walkway or in the driveway.

Although, for a second I thought I caught a hint of something flowery. But it was probably just my imagination.

Chapter 18

"The Purple Flame?" Aislin asked. She was still sitting on the floor of the living room, with the laptop opened up in front of her, the note I found on my bed clasped in her hands.

"Does anyone know what it is?" I asked, hopeful.

All three of them shook their heads.

"Okay...Well, does anyone know how to find out what it is?" I asked, losing some of my hopefulness.

Alex and Aislin exchanged a look.

"What do you think?" Alex asked her. "Do you think it would say anything about it?"

"I don't know...maybe," Aislin deliberated. "But it would be extremely risky....I mean, what if he's there?"

I shot Laylen a *huh* look and he shrugged, like he had no idea what they were talking about either.

"Who's where?" I asked, looking back and forth between Aislin and Alex.

Aislin gave Alex a chary look. "Our house. We would need to go to our house."

My jaw just about smacked against the floor. "You want us to go to your house—to Stephan's house?" Had they lost their minds?

"Maybe...I mean he had that book." Aislin shut the laptop.

"What book?" I asked, totally not on board with this plan. I mean, yeah, I was all for going somewhere that Stephan could possibly be if it meant saving someone's life. But to do it for a book? *A book*?

"History book," Alex said as if it made the situation better, and I raised my eyebrows at him. "A book that outlines the history of the Foreseers."

"And you think this book might know what a Purple Flame is?" I asked, warming up to the idea a little.

"I'm guessing it will." Alex folded his arms and leaned back in the chair. "And it's probably our best bet since we don't have a Foreseer around to help us anymore."

My stomach rolled as I thought of Nicholas. "But, do we dare risk going to your house—to Stephan's house all for a book?"

Alex's face sank as if he had just realized this was a problem.

We all mulled this over, Aislin tapping a pen, Laylen twisting his lip ring, and me tracing the gross olive-green lines on my arm.

"Could you do a Tracker Spell?" I asked Aislin.

She shook her head, still tapping the pen. "My father's immune to magic, remember."

"Oh yeah, I forgot," I mumbled.

Silence.

"I'll go," Alex announced, getting to his feet. "My father never was there anyway, so I doubt he'll be hanging around now."

I jumped to my feet. "No way. It's way too dangerous."

Alex gave me a look that said: look who's being bossy now. "It's okay," he said. "Like I said, he was never there even when we lived there. I think he only came there like twice to check up on us."

"But what if he is?" I stressed, stepping closer to him.

"I can take care of myself, Gemma," he said with a small smile.

"Well, at least let me Foresee us there or something," I said in a panic.

He pressed his lips together, shaking his head. "Can't. There's *Praesidium* everywhere, and besides, you don't know what my place looks like."

I gestured at Aislin. "Well, let Aislin transport you ..."

He was shaking his head. "Can't use magic in the house."

I gaped at him.

"What?" He shrugged. "We lived there, and since we knew about all the things that go bump-in-the-night, we wanted to be protected." He glanced at Aislin and she nodded.

"So what? You're just going to drive there?" I was astounded by the idea.

"Basically, yeah," he said with a shrug. Then he patted me on the shoulder, like I was his buddy or something, an idea which I didn't like. "Don't worry, I already said there's like a one percent chance he'll be there. He never was there—he never was anywhere we were unless it was convenient for him."

I swallowed the giant lump rising in my throat. "Well, at least wait until dark, so he doesn't see you coming if he's there. Plus, there'll be lights on in the house, warning you if he's there."

He nodded. "Alright, I will."

For the rest of the day, we all basically kept to ourselves. Aleesa finally came downstairs and Aislin took her into the kitchen to feed her. She was like a child, in a way, even though she was probably about sixteen. Being in a torture chamber probably had stunted her maturity, like my emotional hollowness had done to me.

I was sitting on the couch, biting at my nails, as Alex prepared to leave.

"I still don't think you should go alone." I tapped my foot nervously. "I should go with you. I mean, I am a Keeper now."

He slipped the knife into the pocket of his jeans and something occurred to him. "You know what; you can go if you want."

I blinked at him. "What?"

He met my eyes. "You're right. You are a Keeper now, and this will be good practice for you—you can be my look out, even though I'm sure my father won't be there—he probably doesn't even know where the house is....I mean, he dropped Aislin and I off to live there and basically bailed."

I stared at him, mystified by his words.

"What? You beg me to let you go, so I do, and now you don't want to go?" he teased.

I gave him an 'oh-shut-up' look. "No, it's just weird that you're letting me go."

"I already said, you're a Keeper now and you can make your own decisions." He leaned in, his breathing picking up. "Besides, you can be our quick exit just in case something happens. All we have to do is get out of the yard and you should have your Foreseer ability."

It was hot in here. When did Afton get so hot?

"Are you about ready to go?" Aislin asked, whisking into the room.

Alex and I jumped back.

"What are you guys doing?" She looked at us displeased as if guilt was written on both our faces.

"Nothing," Alex and I both said quickly.

168

She put her hands on her hips and gave us a skeptical look.

"Gemma's going with me." Alex picked up a small sword off the table and tossed it to me, which I caught effortlessly.

Hmm…I guess being a Keeper wasn't all that bad.

"I don't think that's such a good idea," she protested.

"We'll be fine," Alex assured her. "I really don't think Stephan will be there."

Aislin shook her head. "That's not what I'm worried about. I don't think he'll be there either. He was never there." She paused. "What I'm worried about is you two being alone together in an empty house."

Wow. Way to put it out there.

"We'll be fine," Alex assured her again. "We won't do anything we wouldn't do here." He gave me this weird look that made my skin tingle.

Aislin sighed. "But please hurry. I worry, you know."

"I know…we'll hurry," he said, and we headed out the door.

My car was parked in the driveway, and the keys were in the ignition, just where I always left them. (It's a small town thing). The night air was a bit crisp and I zipped up my purple hoodie.

"Who's driving?" I asked, standing by the driver's side door.

"Um… I will," Alex said, scooting me out of the way. "Since I know where we're going."

I slipped into the passenger seat and buckled my seatbelt. For a while, neither of us spoke. The only sound came from the speakers: "The Quiet Things That No One Ever Knows" by Brand New had popped on when Alex started the engine. I watched the town I grew up in pass by in a blur of colors, the strangest feeling rising up inside me. All these years here, and I barely remember a thing. But, what would there be to remember? Lonely days of wandering. Emptiness.

"Gemma, are you okay?" Alex asked, and I suddenly realized I was crying.

I wiped my tears away. "I have allergies," I lied.

He didn't believe me, but he didn't press further, as if he could sense I was in pain, but it was a pain that was shrinking every day, little by little.

"So what do you think of Aleesa?" I asked, changing the subject away from me.

He shrugged, staring straight ahead at the road. "I don't know…."

Assuming he didn't want to talk about it, I searched my brain for another topic.

"It's just that I can't believe my father did that!" Alex suddenly burst out, gripping the steering wheel tightly. "I mean, first of all, it's not even allowed—for Keepers to mix with fey. And for another thing…" He paused. "He cheated on my mom...she wouldn't have even been gone yet around the time Aleesa was born."

I wasn't sure what to say. "I'm sorry."

He flopped his head back against the headrest in frustration. "Things just keep getting worse and worse...And all because of my father."

"That's not true," I said quietly. "I think this is just as much my father's fault as it is yours'."

His hand gripped the steering wheel tighter. The glow of the pale moon trickled through the window and highlighted the anger in his eyes. "Yeah, well, at least yours' is trying to fix it."

"But why is he?" I chewed on my bottom lip, lost in thought. "I mean, I've been thinking about it, and why the change of heart? My mom said he did it in the first place to gain power like your father, so why did he decide he no longer wanted it?"

"Perhaps being locked away in the Room of Forbidden gave him some time to think about the mistakes he made." Alex tapped his fingers on top of the steering wheel. "Time can make people see things differently...I know it did for me."

I wasn't sure what he was getting at, and I was afraid to ask him because he had that look on his face again, the one where it was as if I were a rose in a garden of weeds.

"I see you differently." His voice was as light as air.

Don't react, my brain screamed, but my heart had other intentions. "That's because I am different."

171

"Yeah, but it's not that. It's something else." He paused, gazing at me intensely, his eyes sparkling even through the dark.

Tell him to stop. "Maybe you see me differently because you understand things now," I offered. "You know what the star's power is for and you don't need to protect me."

"I'll always want to protect you," Alex said, his voice cracking. "No matter what. That will never change."

"But I can take care of myself, you know," I said, keeping my voice steady even though it was extremely difficult. "I mean, I took down a couple of Death Walkers all on my own."

"I know. But it doesn't mean I still don't *want* to protect you," he repeated. His powerful gaze practically burned at my skin.

I let out a gasp from the intensity bursting between us and then immediately felt embarrassed. I turned my head to the window. *Don't blush. Don't blush. Turn it off. You used to do it all the time.*

We remained silent for the rest of the drive. I think we both sensed things were getting a little too intense between us, and if we didn't back off, we might end up doing something stupid.

Alex turned down one of the side roads that weaved into the foothills of the mountains, thick with trees and darkness. Not too far up, he made a sudden sharp turn, dipping the Mitsubishi into the trees.

I grabbed onto the roof, bracing myself against the bumps. "What are you doing?" I cried.

He killed the headlights as he slowed the car to a stop. "I didn't want to pull up, just in case someone is there," he explained and I gave him an incredulous look.

I glanced at the steep hill we were parked on, and the thick trees surrounding us. "You know this doesn't have four-wheel drive, right?" It was a Mitsubishi Mirage for crying out loud.

He smiled and his eyes sparkled in the moonlight. "It'll make it," he assured me.

We got out of the car and crept up the dirt hill. I could barely see, and I found myself wishing that Aislin's see-in-the-dark stuff had been a permanent thing. I did, however, notice that there was a lack of stumbling on my part, which had to be because I was a Keeper now.

At the top of the hill, Alex ducked down, and put his arm in front of me, gesturing for me to stay where I was. I stood as still as a statue as he peered over the hill, then let out a breath of relief.

"I knew no one would be here," he said as he stood up straight.

"The coast is clear?" I asked.

He nodded. "The coast is clear."

We stepped off the hill and onto the driveway. I could make out the outline of Alex's two-story house that blended into the night. When we reached the front door, he slipped his wallet out from his pocket. I gave him a funny

173

look, although I wasn't sure if he could see it through the darkness, and he took out a credit card and held it up.

"I don't have my key on me," he explained. With one quick swipe, he had the door unlocked.

"How many times have you done that before?" I asked as he opened the door.

He shrugged. "A few," he said and stepped inside.

I rolled my eyes and followed him in.

He slipped a flashlight out of his pocket and shined the light around us. "It stinks in here," he murmured. "Like feet."

He was right—there was a foul smell to the air.

"Welcome to my home," Alex muttered, heading for the stairway.

"So where is the book?" I asked in a low voice as I followed him up the stairs.

"In my father's office." He nodded up at the top of the stairs.

I was little surprised when he took me to a room with black and purple checkerboard walls, dark blue carpet, and a massive canopy bed decorated with dark vines and black curtains, that was clearly not an office.

"Whose room is this?" I asked, wishing it were mine

He gave me a smile as he spotlighted the flashlight around. "It's Aislin's."

"No, seriously," I said, unbelieving that the poster of Rise Against hanging on the wall could belong to Aislin. "Whose room is this?"

174

He laughed. "I'm being serious. This is Aislin's room."

I was so confused. "But it's so....so...awesome."

He laughed even harder. "What did you expect it to look like?"

"I don't know....less dark and more....pink and flowery."

He opened the closet. "You have to understand something about Aislin. She's not who she appears to be on the outside. She has a darker side to her." He set the flashlight down and grabbed a box from the top shelf. "Most witches do have a darker side...But my father trained her to be the girl she is on the outside—he controlled her a lot."

He continued to rummage around in the closet, and I walked around the room, still not believing this could be Aislin's room. It just didn't make any sense.

I caught sight of a photo on top of her dresser. I squinted through the darkness at it and realized it was a photo of her and Laylen, sitting out on a porch, smiling for the camera. The sunlight lit up the happiness in their eyes. A happiness which did not exist at the moment.

"What are you looking for?" I walked into the closet beside Alex. "I thought you said the book was in your father's office."

He pulled another box off the top closet shelf—a black one decorated with purple stars—and lifted the lid. "I'm looking for this."

It was a box filled with plastic baggies of herbs, candles, crystals, beads, necklaces, and other stuff I couldn't identify.

"Aislin's witch stuff?" I asked, picking up one of the silver-chained necklaces and examining it.

"Yeah, she figured we could pick it up while we were here."

I nodded and put the necklace back. "It's a good idea. I mean, we've been having to use her magic a lot to help us out."

We left Aislin's room and went into the room across the hall. It was Stephan's office, lined with a ton of shelves that had rows and rows of books.

"Please tell me you know where the Foreseer book is," I said in a hopeful tone.

He shook his head, crushing my hopefulness into smithereens. "Start looking."

A half an hour later, we were up to our elbows in books. Alex had balanced the flashlight in the center of the room, so there was just enough of a faint glow that we could look around. Then we started pulling off books one by one, but none of them were what we were looking for.

"Are you sure the book's in here?" I asked, shutting a book and resting my head against the shelf.

"Yeah, it's in here." Alex scratched his head as he flipped through the pages of a book. "My dad showed it to me during one of the, like, two times he paid us a visit—he said I needed to brush up on my Foreseer knowledge."

"That's a weird thing to say."

He shrugged. "He's always said weird things like that."

I glanced up at the rows and rows of books that still needed to be searched. "Well, what if it's not on the shelf?" I said, getting an idea. "I mean, the book has got to be important, right—if it has the history of the Foreseers in it. So, why would he keep it out in the open?" I paused. "You know, I once went looking for my birth certificate in Marco and Sophia's room."

He looked up from the book he was skimming through, shocked. "Did you find it?"

"Yeah, it was hidden in this secret compartment of this trunk they had." I pointed to a trunk in the corner of the room. "Kind of like that one...."

Alex and I both looked at one another and then we were on our feet, moving for the trunk. Alex swiped the flashlight up from the floor, flipped the latch of the trunk open, and raised the lid. And of course it was full of books—why wouldn't it be? We took them out, checking each one, making sure it wasn't the book we were looking for.

When we reached the bottom, I pushed on the board, and just like the trunk in Marco and Sophia's room, the bottom popped up, and there was our book. I knew right away that it was our book by the eye on the cover. I had

177

seen the same kind of eye on the columns in the place where my father was—the Room of Forbidden. It was an old book with a flimsy cover, worn out from age.

"So this is it." I started to get to my feet, ready to get out of here. But Alex stayed sitting, staring into the trunk.

"What is it?" I glanced in the trunk. "What's wrong?"

He took out a thick leather book with the initials A.A. on it.

"Is it yours?" I asked, figuring A.A. stood for Alex Avery.

He swallowed hard as he flipped through the pages. "I think it's my mother's...journal."

It was a moment for him. I got that. So I stayed quiet while he glanced through it.

He stood up, and his hand holding the flashlight was shaking a little. "I'm taking this with me."

I nodded and helped him pile the books back into the trunk. Then I glanced around at the mess we made. "Should we clean up?" I asked, hoping he would say no.

Alex shook his head, already heading for the door.

And that's when we heard it. A door slamming closed.

The sound dinged through the house, like a warning bell.

Both our eyes widened.

Someone was here.

Chapter 19

"Do you think it's him?" I whispered as Alex clicked the flashlight off.

Darkness.

"I'm not sure." He took my hand, his skin zapping with a static flow. "Be as quiet as possible."

We tiptoed like elves down the hall toward the stairway, but turned right back around when we heard *his* voice drifting up the stairs.

Stephan.

Alex led me into a room and softly clicked the door shut. Then he flipped the flashlight back on. It was his room, I could tell that right away, by all the guy stuff scattered everywhere.

"What are we going to do?" I whispered, my heart knocking into my chest.

He put his finger up to his lips as he walked over to a rug on the floor.

"Are you kidding me?" I shook as he flipped over the rug. Just like I guessed, underneath the rug a square was cut into the hardwood floor. "What is it with you guys and trapdoors?"

"Have you seen the life we live," Alex told me. "Trapdoors are a must." He raised the trapdoor open and shined the light down into the hole.

I was astonished by how small it was inside. "Are we going to be able to fit?"

He rubbed the back of his neck tensely. "I can find someplace else to hide."

Nope. Not going down that road again. "No, we can fit," I assured him and lowered myself into the hole.

It was small. Really, really small. But we managed to squish ourselves into it and with some maneuvering Alex managed to lower the door and get the rug to flop over it.

"Your dad doesn't know where this is, right?" I whispered.

"No," he whispered back, his breath hot on my face. "And I doubt he'll even come in here. I mean, why would he?"

We were laying on our sides, face to face, our legs and arms pressed together. If this wasn't crossing a line, I don't know what was. If we stayed down here for too long, we would kill each other for sure.

Alex turned off the flashlight and everything went dark.

"How do we know when he leaves?" I asked quietly. "And what if he doesn't?"

Alex didn't answer and I knew I worried him. He shifted his body, pressing his legs harder against mine. "Sorry," he said, inching them away.

180

It was growing so electric, I swear, at any moment we were going to turn all 'glow-in-the-dark-like.'

"Maybe we should get out and try to make a run for it," Alex suggested. "Hop out a window or something."

"But if he sees us leaving—"

Alex threw his hand over my mouth. "Shhh...."

I held my breath, my pulse racing as I heard the soft thud of boot's moving across the floor. A *click*—probably the light turning on. The boots paused right above of us and it was so quiet that I didn't dare breathe. The only thing I was grateful for was the fact that the air hadn't chilled, so that meant no Death Walkers were nearby. It was only Stephan, but what was he doing? All I could hear was some fumbling around and then he would stand silently. This went on for quite some time, but then finally the thudding of boots was heading away from us and toward the door. There was a pause and then the door clicked shut.

Neither of us moved. I think we were too afraid he was still in the room; that he knew we were hiding and was trying to trick us to come out. And maybe that's why we stayed in there longer than we probably should have. The electricity kept buzzing and buzzing and I found myself wanting to reach out and touch Alex's face. I was actually starting to feel a little weak, when Alex moved his mouth right next to my ear and whispered, "Stay put. I'll be right back."

181

If I had learned anything at all, stay put meant stay put. So I let him climb out of the hiding spot to go check on things. Although, I wasn't going to lie and say I wasn't worried, especially when I heard the sounds of footsteps thumping against the floorboards above me. They paused for a few moments, and I waited for Stephan to throw open the door and say: 'Ah! I found you.'

But it was Alex's face that appeared when the trapdoor lifted open. I handed him the book and his mom's journal, and then heaved myself out.

"Do you think he knew someone was here?" I asked.

Alex shook his head, his forehead creasing over with puzzlement. "I don't think so...but why did he come here...and in my room?" He glanced around the room, his eyes landing on the top dresser drawer, which was open.

Alex handed me the flashlight and dug around inside the drawer. "Why would he...I don't get it?"

"What's missing?" I asked, pointing the flashlight at the inside of the drawer.

He shook his head. "My mirror."

"Like your make-up mirror," I joked, and then pressed my lips together when he gave me a dirty look. "Sorry."

He shook his head. "No, it's just...I don't get it—why did he take it?"

"Was there something special about the mirror?" I asked.

182

He shut the drawer. "I don't know...I got it from a witch who told me it would show me my future if I looked in it, but it was a bunch of crap because every time I looked in it all I saw was light."

I dropped the flashlight. "You saw what?"

"Light." He picked up the flashlight and shined it in my eyes. "You okay?"

"Yeah, I'm fine." I blinked against the bright light. "But maybe your father's worried that we changed the future and he thought this mirror would show him."

"Maybe..." Alex looked at me strangely, knowing there was something else wrong.

"We should probably go in case he comes back." I started for the door, figuring he would argue, but he didn't.

Alex was right: my Mitsubishi did make it off the hill. After a little bit of backing up, and some spinning of the tires, we were driving down the road. Alex hadn't said a word since we had left his house. And that was okay. I was too distracted by what he had told me about the light. I worried that there might be a connection there, between what he saw in the mirror and what I kept seeing repeatedly every time my eyes closed.

I started reading through the pages of the Foreseers' book. The first few chapters were pretty boring, but then I stumbled onto something interesting.

The Room of Forbidden: A desolate place where no soul lives except the seer that committed the crime. In the Room of Forbidden, the seer will spend an eternity alone. No one can enter the Room of Forbidden, for the room exists only in the seer's mind.

"The Seer's mind," I didn't mean to say it out loud.

"What?" Alex cast a quick glance at me, somewhat distracted.

"It's nothing." I waved him off. But I couldn't understand how my dad was stuck in a room inside his own head. And that I was in there once.

I shivered and went back to my reading.

The power of a Foreseer's mind: The Foreseer's mind is one of the most powerful tools. In fact, some of the more powerful Foreseers are able to push their minds to see what they need to see in times of great need.

Push the mind to see what it needs to see in times of great need? Hmm...I wondered how that one worked. I turned the page, hoping for detailed instructions, but the only thing there was a drawing of a person with an eye on the center of their forehead. I touched my figure to my forehead, wondering what it meant.

I went on skimming through the pages, looking for the words "purple" or "flame," but by the time Alex pulled in the driveway, I still hadn't found a mention of either.

Alex killed the engine and turned to me. "Hey, can we keep what happened back at the house a secret? I don't want to worry Aislin more than she already is...she's been really stressed out lately."

I actually thought this was a good idea. "Yeah, I'll keep it to myself."

He gave me a small smile and we went inside the house. Aislin was sitting at the kitchen table, a bunch of herbs and leaves scattered in front of her, along with a few candles.

"Did you get the book?" she asked as soon as we stepped over the threshold.

I nodded, lifting up the Foreseers' book. "Yep, we got it."

"Run into any problems?" She was distracted with her herbs and didn't notice when I glanced at Alex.

"No, everything went fine." Alex slipped off his jacket and hung it on the back of the chair. Then he sat the box of herbs that we had picked up from Aislin's room onto the table "Did you run into any problems here?"

She shook her head, turning a page of the book she was reading. "Everything's fine. Jocelyn's asleep, and Laylen's showing Aleesa what a TV is."

I slid down into a chair at the table. "What are you doing with all this stuff?" I picked up a red and green leaf and turned it in my fingers.

"I am trying to finger out a spell that will remove the mark." She turned the page of the book.

I put the leaf back on the table. "Is that the book you...borrowed from Medea's?"

185

"Um…yeah." She peered up at me with a guilty smile.

I thought about her room and when I saw her shoplift. There seemed to be more to Aislin then what I had originally thought.

"You got that book from Medea's?" Alex picked up the book and turned it to the back cover.

Aislin tried to grab it back, but Alex moved it behind his back. "I don't think you should be doing any spells from this thing," he said. "If it's from Medea's store."

"It's just something she was selling, Alex." Aislin held out her hand impatiently. "Now give it back."

Alex shook his head. "No, not until you promise me you won't do any of the spells in it."

"Fine," she agreed, but I had a feeling she was lying. "Now give it back."

He handed the book back to her, and she sat it on her lap. She reached over and grabbed the box of herbs and starting digging through it.

I let out a yawn, and my eyelids suddenly felt very heavy. "I'm going to bed," I said.

Alex glanced up at the clock. "It's pretty early for bed."

"Yeah, but it's been a long day that used a lot of my energy." I gave him a pressing look so he would understand what I meant. Our little trapdoor incident had drained me dry and I was actually starting to feel some consequences.

186

"Well, goodnight then," Alex said, pretending he had no idea what my look meant.

I sighed and got to my feet. I could barely keep my eyes open as I dragged myself up to bed. I was out before my head even hit the pillow.

Chapter 20

Light. Light everywhere.

"It'll be all right," Alex whispered, bushing my hair out of my face. "I want to protect you forever."

The lake water crackled with ice, and death seized the air as the light blinded me.

"It'll be alright," Alex whispered again and I clutched onto him tightly as the light suffocated me.

Images of my surroundings flipped through my mind like a picture show: Death Walkers...Stephan....fire.

Then, nothing but ash.

"Wake up," someone mumbled. "Come on, open your eyes." A hand touched my arm.

Someone was in my room.

My eyes shot open, and with one swift movement I shoved the person down and was on my feet, preparing to attack.

"Gemma," Aislin hissed from the floor. "Calm down, it's just me."

I clicked the lamp on and I blinked down at her. "I'm so sorry." I helped her to her feet.

"It's okay." She was wearing pajama bottoms with little pink hearts on them and a pink hoodie. "Were you having a nightmare or something?"

"Or something," I mumbled, thinking of the light vision and how I couldn't seem to get rid of it. And where had the fire and ash suddenly come from?

"Gemma….you know you can talk to me about stuff," she said, smoothing out her hair. "I can be a really good listener if you'll give me a chance."

I thought of her room and wondered if we had more in common than I knew. "Okay, I might take you up on that." I noticed she had her purse on. "Are you going somewhere?"

She nodded, looking guilty. "And you are too….I mean, if you'll help me that is?"

"Help you with what?" I asked with interest.

"A spell…"

"From the book you…borrowed."

"Yeah, and I know Alex told me not to do any spells out of it, but I found one that might work."

I took my hoodie off the back of the computer chair. "To remove the Mark of Malefiscus?"

"Yeah." She took the book out of her purse and flipped it open. "The Spell of Zaleena."

I squinted down at the page and pulled a face. "It looks…interesting." On the page was a drawing of a woman, her head tilted back, her hands spread out to the side of

189

her. Normal, right? Except that her mouth was open and a spirit was rising out of it.

"So you think this spell's going to remove the Mark of Malefiscus?" I asked as she slid the book back into her purse.

"The spell's not exactly for removing a mark." She zipped up her purse. "But it's supposed to give the witch who performs the spell the gift of being able to separate and remove evil from those who are naturally good."

I put my hoodie on and zipped it up. "Yeah, I can see why you would think it might work, but....it's not dangerous, right?"

"I don't think so..." She seemed uncertain. "It shouldn't be, but when it comes to magic, you never know."

A pause.

"You don't have to come if you don't want to," she said. "I mean, I get it if you don't, but I think your energy might come in real handy because it's a really powerful spell...And I could use your company."

"Alright, I'm in," I said. "So, where are we going?"

Nervousness rose on her face. "The cemetery."

Never in a million years would I have thought I would be wandering down the street, late at night, with a witch, heading to a cemetery. I felt like I had stepped into a ghost story or something.

The cemetery was located at the edge of the forest. The moon was a bright orb against the pitch black sky, clouds moving whimsically in front of it. The air was hauntingly silent and still, except for the crunching of gravel underneath our shoes.

"So...how intense is this spell going to be?" I asked, trying to break the silence before it drove me insane.

"Honestly?" she asked, and I nodded. "Probably pretty difficult."

Silence filled the air between us again, and I fidgeted with the zipper of my hoodie as I searched for something else to say to her.

"Gemma," she sputtered abruptly. "Do you like Laylen?"

"*What*? Like as friends?" I asked, even though I was sure she didn't mean it that way.

She shook her head, and the uneasiness could be seen in her expression even through the darkness. "I mean, like...more than as friends...like maybe the same way as you do with Alex." She held her breath, waiting for me to answer.

I felt extremely uncomfortable in the vacant streets, covered by nighttime shadows. The prickle poked at the back of my neck, but I was unsure what emotion was trying to surface.

"Laylen and I are just friends," I told her, but something felt wrong about the answer.

191

She sidestepped around a lamppost. "It's just that sometimes you two seem....I don't know. You just seem happier when you're around each other."

Were we? "Yeah, I guess..." It felt like I needed to say something here; something that would make her feel better. "I think that's just because we're comfortable around each other. I mean, Laylen has always been honest with me, which makes things easier with him."

She nodded, looking hurt, and I wondered if I said the wrong thing. "Gemma, I'm sorry for lying to you...but I think if you'll give me another chance, you and I could be really good friends."

Friends. God, the word was so foreign to me, but I didn't want it to be anymore. "Yeah, I would like that."

She looked relieved. "Good, I'm glad."

I wondered if she was referring to us being friends or to the fact that I said Laylen and I were just friends.

Suddenly, something stomped on the ground behind us and we both spun around, searching through the dark, but there was nothing there.

"Weird..." Aislin muttered as we turned back around.

"So just how dangerous is this going to be?" I asked, changing the subject. "The spell, I mean."

She didn't answer right away, pulling her jacket tighter. "I'm not sure..."

I wrapped my arms around myself as I shivered. "But you don't think it will be like zombies-will-raise-out-of-the-ground dangerous, do you?"

She gave me a tense smile. "I don't think so."

The cemetery rose into view and goose-bumps dotted my arms. It was a small cemetery, sealed up by an iron gate. A few trees trimmed around the edge and a gravel path ran up the center.

"I think—"

Another thump came up from behind us, this time much louder and closer. Aislin slipped a knife out of her purse and we both spun around again, preparing to kick whatever's butt was behind us.

A girl stood there, dressed in a pink plaid pajama set, wide eyed and terrified.

Aleesa.

She let out a shriek that cut through the quiet air around us.

"Stop!' Aislin covered Aleesa's mouth. "Shhh…it's okay."

Aislin and I exchanged a worried glance.

"What are you doing here?" Aislin asked, lowering her hand.

"I saw you leaving from out the window," Aleesa said, her yellow eyes still bulging with fear. "And I followed you….I wanted to come with you."

Aislin frowned unhappily. She grabbed my arm and turned us away from Aleesa.

"What should we do with her?" she whispered.

I glanced over my shoulder at Aleesa and shrugged. "Take her with us, I guess."

"I don't know..." Aislin looked at Aleesa with uncertainty.

"What else are we going to do?" I asked. "Take her back? The sun will be coming up in like an hour and I'm pretty sure we don't want to be sitting out in the cemetery performing a witch spell when it does."

"Yeah...I guess you're right." She motioned at Aleesa. "Come on, you can come with us."

Aleesa actually looked a little happy for a second, her yellow eyes flickering like two fireflies as she skipped after us.

We made it the rest of the way to the cemetery without any more bumps in the night. Aislin said we had to find a fresh grave, which totally freaked me out. But I still wandered through the dark, helping her look for one, with Aleesa trailing along quietly behind us. We finally found one at the back of the cemetery in the midst of the darkest shadows beneath a giant oak tree.

Aislin took some black and red candles out of her purse and placed them on the ground in a circle.

"Alright, now we just need to sit in a circle around the candles," she said, the glow of the flames lighting up the serious expression on her face.

I sat down on the cold ground of the cemetery and so did Aislin and Aleesa. Aislin sprinkled a black powder over the candles, making the flames shift from a bright orange to a deep red. Then she took out the book.

"Okay," she muttered, placing a red and green leaf in the center of the candles. "Are you guys ready for this?"

Aleesa nodded eagerly, but she had no idea what was going on here. I nodded with less eagerness and Aislin took a deep breath.

"*EGO dico ut maleena ut orior oriri ortus iterum,*" Aislin chanted under her breath.

Aleesa watched her with big eyes as Aislin continued to chant this over and over again. I, however, was restless. For some reason, I kept getting this feeling that someone was watching us. My eyes kept scanning the dark, and again I wished the night vision thing had been permanent. Each time I looked I couldn't see anyone, but I couldn't shake the uneasy feeling.

"*EGO dico ut maleena ut orior oriri ortus iterum!*" Aislin screamed, bringing me back to what we were doing.

The candles' flames had shifted to a yellow-black, casting an eerie glow across Aislin's face, as if she were possessed. Then, suddenly the flames burst and began to entwine together, until they were one giant black flame.

My mouth dropped as the flame formed the shape of a woman, who rose above us and opened her hollow eyes.

""*EGO dico ut maleena ut orior oriri ortus iterum!*" Aislin screamed again and I worried someone was going to hear us and call the cops.

And then, to add to the noise factor, flame woman decided to let out a deafening wail.

Aleesa screamed as she jumped to her feet in a fearful panic. Aislin's eyes and my eyes snapped wide as Aleesa took off running through the cemetery heading for the iron gate.

I glanced from the flaming woman to Aislin, hesitating, wondering if Aislin needed me or if I should go chase Aleesa down.

"Go get her!" Aislin cried, her hands out to the side of her, her eyes locked on the flame woman. "I'll be fine!"

I casted one last look at the flame woman and then I was on my feet, charging through the night, my DCs hammering against the ground as I zigzagged around the headstones dotting the graveyard.

"Where did she go?" I muttered, searching the darkness as I ran. Then, I spotted her climbing over the fence, and I sped up, running faster than I ever thought was possible. With one quick leap, I was up and over the fence.

For a split second, I stood there stunned, blinking back at the fence I had just jumped over. Did I seriously just do that? I shook my head—that was beside the point—and scanned the road to my left, then right, but nothing. No Aleesa.

Crap. Okay, if I were Aleesa, where would I go? I had no idea how to answer my question, so I took off to my right, since it was the way to the house. As I barreled around the corner at full speed, I slammed into something that almost knocked me to the ground. I shook off my stumble, figuring it was Aleesa. But when I looked up, my heart stopped.

He was tall, with skin as pale as snow, his eyes as black as the night sky. He sized me up with his dark eyes and then smiled.

My heart stopped.

Sharp, shiny fangs.

A vampire.

Chapter 21

"Why, hello there," the vampire purred, stepping toward me. He was dressed head-to-toe in black and his bleach blond hair was gelled back. The scent of rust and salt flowed off him. "I think I've ran into a bit of luck, haven't I?"

Luck. Just what kind of luck was he talking about?

I started to back away. But the vampire followed my movement, taking a step toward me every time I inched back, as if we were dancing. He pushed up the sleeve of his long-sleeve black shirt, preparing to do who knows what to me. My jaw dropped at the Mark of Malefiscus tracing up the back of his hand. Same mark, different spot, but I'm sure it meant the same thing.

First the witch, Medea, and now a vampire. The Mark of Malefiscus was showing up everywhere.

"Didn't you know that wandering around at night is a dangerous thing?" He nodded at the cemetery gate. "Especially at a place like this." His fangs glinted in the moonlight and his eyes were as dark as death.

I needed to do something quick to get myself out of this situation. I could Foresee my way back to the house, but what kind of person would I be to bail on Aislin like that. I racked my brain, trying to remember how to kill a vampire. Stake to the heart? Yeah, I didn't have one of those. But I was a Keeper now, so there had to be a way, right? I found myself thinking: what would Alex do in this situation?

Before I could conjure up an answer, the vampire lunged for me, and with one swift movement I kicked him right between the legs. Okay, that probably wasn't what Alex would have done, but it worked. The vampire collapsed to the ground, and taking advantage of his momentary weakness, I moved to jump back over the fence. But the vampire grabbed my ankle and dragged me back down. I tripped forward and smacked my head onto the iron fence.

I saw stars and not just in the sky. I blinked. Focus, Gemma. *Foresee your way to Aislin.*

I shut my eyes and focused on the graveyard, but then the vampire sank its teeth into my leg. Without even thinking, I grabbed a nearby stick off the ground, turned and stuck it in the vampire's back. Blood. Ashes. More stars. Alex. Then, blackness engulfed me.

I woke up with a killer headache and my leg burned so badly it felt like it was on fire. It was light outside, the sun sparkling warmly against my back. How long had I been out? I pushed myself up to my feet and immediately shut my eyes against the stingingly bright light.

"Do you see it?" a muffled voice asked.

I squinted behind me, looking for someone in the light.

"Look for it, Gemma," the voice urged. "Look past the light."

"Dad?" I asked. "Is that you?"

Silence.

"Hello," I called out, taking a blind step forward.

"Gemma," the voice appeared again. "Focus your mind...see past the light."

This time I knew the voice was my dad's. I focused my eyes, only to be blinded in return by the light.

"Open your mind," he commanded. "Let it see what it needs to see...let it see past the obvious"

It reminded me of a page in the Foreseers' book, about the mind showing me what I needed to see in times of great need. I let my eyes relax, along with my body, and let my Foreseer power take over. The light shifted dark, and then flickered like a strobe light, before fading away completely.

I was standing in the center of Main Street in Afton. It was dark and shadowed by heavy fog, and the buildings, which once had life, were dead and broken and burning with fire. The sky was black, the moon full. Painful cries filled the cold air and there was the smell of death nearby.

A vampire darted past me, fangs out, eyes black, the Mark of Malefiscus on his arm. He moved up to a figure that stepped out of the building's shadows. The figure's dark hair matched his dark eyes and the fire that blazed up and down the street lit up the scar on his left cheek.

Stephan.

"Good work," Stephan said to the vampire, his eyes glowing like coals in the bright orange glow of the fires. "I see this is all working out."

The vampire hissed through his fangs in delight. "Just as you wanted."

Stephan glanced up and down the streets, smiling at the chaos. "Yes, exactly as I wanted."

The picture slowly faded and I stood there waiting for my dad to speak again.

"Do you understand, Gemma?" His voice floated all around me. "Do you understand what this means?"

I shook my head. "I thought the world ended in ice, not fire...Is this before the Death Walkers freeze everything over? Is this when the witches, vampires, and fey come out?"

"You have to understand," he said. "You need to prepare yourself."

Why did he always have to tiptoe around the details? "Dad, I don't get what you're saying...I don't get any of this. Why did I see the world ending in fire...And how am I supposed to get into the mapping ball you gave me?"

The light flickered and I drifted away.

"Dad," I called out, willing my mind to stay longer. "Please tell me what to do...I need to know what to do."

"You will know in time," his voice echoed after me. "You have to figure it out on your own. Just remember to let your mind see what it needs to see....let it see past what's in front of you."

Before I could say anything else, I was gone.

Chapter 22

When I opened my eyes again the sun was ascending over the mountains, and sparkling the valley with hues of pink and orange. I blinked against the morning sky as I pushed myself to my feet. There was no sign of the vampire anywhere, but a pile of black ash stained the gravel.

I stretched out my back and headed across the cemetery to look for Aislin, trying not to think about the disturbing image I had seen, or my father's unsettling words.

Aislin ended up being exactly where I left her. She was gathering up her candles, looking rather pleased, which I took as a good sign that the spell had worked.

But when she caught sight of me, her pleased looked slipped into a frown. "You didn't find her."

I gave her a funny look. "Who...Oh! Aleesa." I shook my head. "I completely forgot." I turned around, preparing to leave to go search for Aleesa.

"Wait, Gemma," Aislin called after me. "Why is your leg bleeding?"

I glanced at my leg, scarred with the bloody marks of vampire fangs. Then I let out a heavy sigh and told her what happened.

"So you saw the streets burning and my father was there?" Aislin asked as we walked the streets, looking for Aleesa.

I nodded. "I almost wondered if, you know, it was like the prequel to the ice vision I saw—the one in Vegas where the streets were empty and frozen over...I'm not sure though....especially since my dad said I needed to prepare myself."

Aislin let out a shudder as we crossed the street. "God, what if that's what it means—what if that's what actually happens?"

"I don't know...But, if anything, seeing that makes me want to get into the mapping ball quicker."

We hopped over the curb and started across the park's lawn, hoping to spot Aleesa.

"I don't think she's here." Aislin sighed worriedly. "Where would she go?"

I shook my head, worried about Aleesa too. She was so new to everything and I feared something might happen to her. But I was also worried about what my father had said—that I needed to prepare myself. I mean, was he doubting I could save the world? I let out a frustrated sigh. Why couldn't he just give me a straight answer?

"Who is that?" Aislin asked.

204

I followed her gaze to a car pulling up in front of the park. "Ah, crap."

Aislin's face dropped. "Wait, is that your car?"

It was indeed a Mitsubishi Mirage. The door opened up and Alex stepped out, looking pissed. At first I thought it was because we had snuck out of the house, but then I saw a pair of bright yellow eyes peer at us from the passenger-side window.

"Did you two lose something?" he asked, his hands tucked in his pockets as he walked across the lawn toward us.

Aislin let out a guilty laugh. "Where did you find her?"

Alex shook his head, annoyed. "She came running into the house, screaming at the top of her lungs." He paused in front of us. "When I got her to calm down, she told me you two were at the cemetery and that there was a crying fire woman there."

"Hmmm...that's weird," I said, trying to keep Aislin from getting a lecture. "Maybe she imagined it."

"It's okay, Gemma," Aislin said, then fixed her eyes determinedly on Alex. "Yes, we were at the cemetery doing a spell which is going to hopefully remove the Mark of Malefiscus."

"I told you not to use that book," Alex said flatly.

"Well, you know what, I used it," Aislin said with a fire in her voice. "And I'm glad I did because the spell just might have worked....I just need to try it out..." Aislin

205

looked at me. "I would like to try it out on your mom, but I understand if you want me to find another person with the Mark of Malefiscus."

"Yeah, because those are easy to come by," Alex interrupted.

"Easier than you might think," I said. When he gave me a confused look, I told him about the vampire as we headed for the car.

"So, you were bit by another vampire?" Alex asked, his eyes burning wildly with rage. "Gemma—"

I covered his mouth with my hand. "It's okay, I killed it, everything's good." I lowered my hand, shivering from the sparks that flowed at my fingertips. "Besides, we have much bigger problems to deal with."

By the time we made it home, a nervous tension was bearing down on us.

"So what do you think it means?" Alex asked. "That you're not going to be able to save the world?"

We were parked in the driveway. Aislin climbed out, eager to go and try her newfound power on my mom, and Aleesa followed in after her.

I gripped the door handle. "Oh, I'm going to save the world," I assured him with an alarming amount of confidence. "I'm going to go up to my room and read that book from cover to cover until I find out how to get a hold of this Purple Flame."

He gave me an intense look that made me squirm in my skin.

"What?" I asked, shaking my head at the breathlessness of my voice.

He shrugged. "It's nothing, it's just that you have this take charge attitude...and I kind of like it."

I made no reaction as I opened my door. "Well, you need to stop looking at me like that."

He kept looking at me the same way. "I'll try, but I can't promise anything."

I tried not to smile, because I knew it was wrong, but as I turned my back to him to climb out of the car, I couldn't do anything but smile.

I did exactly what I said and went up to my room to look through the Foreseers' book. Aislin was in with my mother, who had been more than willingly to help test Aislin's spell experiment. Aislin said it might take a while to get her new power to work correctly, but once she did she would let me know if it worked. All I could do was cross my fingers that it would, not only for my mom's sake, but for the sake of others as well. I mean, who knew how many people Stephan had marked against their will.

But things weren't going very well. Aislin tried all day to get the power to work, without getting any results. By the time day had crept into the late hours of the night, she was drained dry and decided to get some rest and try again tomorrow.

But even after the house had settled into its deep sleep, I was still awake, reading through the Foreseers' book, which seemed to be going on and on. Finally I tossed the book on the floor in frustration.

"Why can't I find what I need..." I trailed off as I stared at the Foreseers' book opened up on the floor. *The Power of a Foreseer's Mind.*

Suddenly, I had an idea. I shut my eyes and focused all my attention on seeing what I needed. But all I could see was light. *See past the light, see what you need to see.* The Purple Flame...the Purple Flame...the...Purple...

I was energized, glowing. I could feel the energy in me, about to burst like an erupting volcano.

"Open your eyes, Gemma" a familiar voice whispered.

I obeyed and opened my eyelids. The massive crystal ball, in the center of the City of Crystal, burned in front of me, bright like the sun. People were strapped to it, tubes embedded in their skin, feeding energy to the massive ball.

"What you need is not in the book, Gemma," the voice purred softly in my ear. "It's in there. Touch it and you'll see."

I glanced at the crystal ball nervously as I stepped slowly toward it. Taking a deep breath, I reached my trembling hand out to the glowing ball. It seemed to magnetize to me, or I to it, pulling and pulling and pulling me toward it, begging us to connect. And when I placed my palm on it, a fire lit up inside me. My pulse raced as energy whipped through my body. I was charged—powerful. I pulled back, breathing heavily at the sight of the Purple Flame burning in the palm of my hand.

The Purple Flame.

"One of these days, you're going to have to figure things out without me," the voice said and this time I recognized the voice completely.

I turned around. "Nicholas…"

But the only thing there was the lingering smell of flowers.

My eyes shot open and I bolted upright, lifting my hand in front of me. There was no fire burning in it. But I knew what the answer was. I knew what I had to do.

I put my shoes on and grabbed the Traveler's Ball that had been left on my bed, figuring it was probably best to enter the city the correct way. Then I shut my eyes, and a few seconds later, I was gone.

Chapter 23

I landed with the gracefulness of a cat, and I touched my finger to my shoulder blade, feeling a temporary moment of happiness for the mark. I was standing at the entrance of the cave where the red rubies waved across the snow-white crystal wall and dark red crystals pointed down from the glittering charcoal ceiling. I immediately took off towards where I knew the massive crystal ball burned bright, my feet softly thudding against the translucent crystal floor that covered the flowing midnight river. I ran past the area where Laylen had knocked Nicholas out once, and charged by where Alex, Laylen and I had made our escape from the Death Walkers. I reached the pair of silver doors with the Foreseers' mark on top and slipped quietly into the room.

My stomach instantly rolled at the sight of the bodies strapped to the giant crystal. Just like the first time I had been here, their eyes were still shut, their bodies still slack with tubes sticking out of their skin.

I walked towards the massive crystal ball, shining so brightly it hurt my eyes. Yet I didn't look away. I held my breath and tried to block out the human bodies on each side of me as I leaned forward and put my hand to the crystal. Energy zapped through my body and my heart sped up so fast I thought it was going to explode out of my chest. I couldn't breathe. It was too much. I yanked my hand back and gasped at the sight of the Purple Flame burning in the palm of my hand.

I did it by myself. I took pride in this fact; a kind of pride I had never felt before.

Instinctively I shut my hand, and the flame *poofed* out. I opened it again and Ta-da! the flame ignited.

"Wow," I muttered under my breath. I opened and closed my hand a few more times, watching in awe at the sight of the Purple Flame lighting up and smothering out. But, finally, I decided I better leave. I could play with the flame when I got back. I shut my hand, suffocating the flame, and headed to the door, slipping the Traveler's Ball out of my pocket. I had been warned once not to use the power of the Divination Crystal so close to the massive crystal ball that supplied all the energy, so I figured I would wander a ways back down the hall before I took myself home.

I cast one last glance back at the people strapped to the crystal ball, their energy being sucked from them. One day, I would come down here and free them all, even if it meant there would be no more Foreseers. The world could live without Foreseers. I mean, look at what my father had done.

I turned back to the door just as it swung open and smacked me in the face. The Traveler's Ball slipped from my fingers and crashed against the floor, breaking into pieces of glass and rubies.

"Crap." It was a good thing I had a backup.

A man entered the room wearing a silver robe that matched his sliver eyes. His skin was pale, his hair grey, and I had seen him before.

"Gemma?" Dyvinius said, startled by the sight of me. "What are you doing in here?"

"A...um...would you believe me if I said I was lost?" I said innocently.

He stared at me blankly, either not getting or not appreciating my sense of humor.

"Sorry." I deliberated my options. I could go all ninja on him; I mean, I was a Keeper now. But kicking an old guy's butt didn't seem right. So I let three seconds tick by, and then I ran.

My shoes skidded against the crystal floor as I barreled around the massive crystal ball. I wasn't sure what to do. Did I dare risk using my power so close to a crystal loaded with power?

"Gemma." Dyvinius' voice came from right behind me. Wow, he was quick for an old guy.

I decided the heck with it and shut my eyes. It was definitely time to go. But I couldn't feel it; there was no power. Had the Purple Flame sucked the power out of me?

"There's no use trying, Gemma," Dyvinius said, in his monotone-like voice. "I have the place on lockdown. No one may leave or enter, even with a unique Foreseer gift like yours."

Chapter 24

So Dyvinius knew about my gift. Why did this seem like such a bad thing? Oh, yeah, because it probably was.

And what was this lockdown business?

I opened my eyes, telling myself to stay calm. "What do you mean you have it on lockdown? And how do you know about...my gift?"

He gave me a small smile, which looked creepy on his unemotional face. "You are your father's daughter, aren't you? How could I not know?" He turned around, his silver robe swishing lightly across the crystal floor. "This way please. We have much to talk about."

Having no choice but to follow, I trudged along after him as he walked out the door and down the translucent crystal path. He led me over the bridge paved with bits of broken porcelain, underneath the pillars, and through the tall, silver doors, saying nothing to me the entire time. The longer we walked, the more worried I became. What if he wouldn't let me go? Or worse, what if he let me go, but took the Purple Flame away from me?

When we reached his silver throne perched upon the blue sapphire podium, he took a seat and stared at me heavily with his silver eyes.

"Gemma, I'm not sure if you fully understand our laws," he finally said. "But we have certain rules to which Foreseer's are supposed to abide to. The first and most important being never tamper with visions." He paused, placing his hands on his lap and overlapping his fingers. "I'm not sure if you're aware of this or not, but your father broke this law a long time ago."

"You know who my father is?" I fidgeted around anxiously.

"How could I not?" he said with a blank tone. "You look so much like him."

Absentmindedly, I touched the corner of my eye. "Why didn't you say you did the first time you met me?"

"Because, back then you weren't who you are now," Dyvinius said with a glint in his silver eyes. "I see you heading down the same road as your father did."

I wondered if by "see" he actually meant *see*. "What road?" I played dumb.

He leaned forward in his throne. "Has anyone told you what happened to your father?"

"No," I lied, wanting to hear his side of the story.

"Well, he was a lot like you in the sense of his power," Dyvinius explained, not looking very happy. "He could use the power of the Divination Crystal beyond the

215

boundaries of an average Foreseer, beyond what even I can do."

Hmm…What was he getting at here?

"Your father has done some unforgivable things." Dyvinius paused, considering something. "And because of that, he will forever pay—he will forever be a prisoner in the Room of Forbidden, alone in his own mind."

I shivered, still a little shocked by the idea that the Room of Forbidden was actually a place in his mind. I had been in my father's mind. But I assumed that Dyvinius did not know about this.

"Changing visions is a dangerous thing, Gemma." Dyvinius curled his pale, thin fingers around the edge of the arms of the throne. "And there is severe punishment for it."

Punishment? As in the Room of Forbidden? But how could this apply to changing a vision back to what it was to begin with? How could it apply when I would be saving the world? God, I hoped it didn't apply, or else I would end up stuck in my own head, just like my father.

"Now, I hope you will take what I said and obey the laws." His silver gaze bore into me. "I wouldn't want you to end up like you father."

"I won't end up like him," I assured him, hoping it was true.

"Good." Dyvinius seemed pleased, but it was hard to tell for sure since the man hardly showed emotion. "You may go." He gestured toward the tall, silver doors.

I didn't even question why he was letting me go. I turned around and headed down the porcelain path for the tall, silver doors. It took all my willpower not to take off in a mad sprint.

"Oh yes, and, Gemma," Dyvinius called out.

I stopped, but didn't turn around.

"I look forward to the day when you come back for your training," he said in a way that made me wonder if he thought I wasn't coming back.

When I returned back to the house, Alex was awake, reading his mother's journal. I didn't know how long I had been gone, but enough time passed that the sun was rising up from behind the mountains and softly kissing everything with light.

I don't think Alex would have even realized I had been gone if I hadn't Foreseed my way into the living room instead of my room, something that was entirely done by accident because I had been using my power a little too much and my weakened state was making me lose some of my control.

My sudden appearance in the middle of the living room scared him so badly he actually leapt to his feet and reached for his knife that was on the coffee table. But once his brain processed it was me, he relaxed. That is, until he realized my sudden appearance meant I had snuck away somewhere.

"What...Where have you..." He was pushing on the verge of a freak-out, but struggling to control it.

Hmm...what would be the best way to handle the situation?

I opened my hand and the Purple Flame ignited.

His face froze in shock, but the anger left. "Where...how did you..."

I put out the flame, sat down on the couch, and started to explain.

"You saw Nicholas?" It was the first thing Alex asked when I finished my story.

"No. I didn't see him. But Nicholas' voice was there...he told me what to do."

"Why didn't you wake me up?" Alex sat on the couch across from me, looking both hurt and irritated. "Why didn't you take me to the City of Crystal with you?"

I shrugged. "I'm not sure...I guess I just thought it was something I should do on my own." I paused. "And I think you and I needed a little break from one another."

Okay, he no longer looked hurt, just pissed. "You think we need a break from each other?"

"I didn't mean it like that," I said quickly. "It's just that...didn't you feel a little...weird after we got out of the hiding spot at your house?"

He gave be a blank stare. "I didn't feel anything at all."

"Don't be like that," I said in a sharp tone and then added a polite, "Please."

218

He continued to give me the same blank stare, but I could see the struggle flickering in his eyes. He was trying to turn it back on...his emotions, instead of being the old uncaring Alex. And then, suddenly, it flipped on like a light switch, and the look he gave me made me want to run up to my room—I should run up to my room.

"Have you ever thought about what you're going to do, after you fix the vision and everything goes back to normal?" he asked, leaning over the coffee table toward me.

My heart knocked in my chest. "I'm still not even sure if I can...I mean, I don't even know what's going to be waiting for me in the mapping ball."

He smiled softly. "I'm sure you'll figure it out. You've done a lot of things that seem hard at first."

I gave him a strange look. Where was this coming from?

He got up from the couch and took a seat beside me.

"Alex, I don't think—"

He cut me off. "Just give me a second. I promise I'll back off before things get too intense, but I have to say something, okay?"

I nodded, my voice barely a whisper. "Okay."

He sat silently for a moment, running his fingers through his dark brown hair as he deliberated his words. "You know, you and I are the same, I think."

I gave him a *duh* look and gestured between us, at the invisible electricity flowing between us. "Well, obviously."

219

He smiled amusedly, getting what I meant. "But that's not what I'm talking about." He shifted in his seat, his knee bumping into mine for a split second, but it was enough to send a shockwave of heat through my body. "I mean, we're the same in the sense of how we think."

"I don't..." I furrowed my eyebrows. Was I...like Alex?

He continued to struggle to put his feelings into words; I could tell because it was something I often did. Okay, so maybe we were kind of the same.

"I mean, we're the same in the way we think," he finally said, letting out a loud breath. "Like for instance, how neither one of us thinks about the future." He paused, waiting for me to tell him if he was correct or not—if I thought about my future.

And this sad and unsettling feeling passed over me as I realized I hadn't—not really anyway. I had never pictured what I would be, where I would go, or what I would do.

"I don't," I said, shocked by this sudden revelation. "I don't think about my future."

"Neither have I, really." Alex flopped back in the sofa, his face twisted with confusion. "All my life I've focused on one thing...and that was being the Keeper my father wanted me to be."

I slowly leaned back against the sofa, my brain running a million miles a second. What would I do when this was all over? What would I do if I saved the world? What would I do with my life?

"We could go somewhere," he said, meeting my eyes. "You and I."

I raised my eyebrows. "Just you and me?"

He cocked an eyebrow at me. "Why so doubting? Think about it. You put the vision back to what it was, and we no longer have to worry about my father playing out his crazy world-ending plan and you and I can actually do whatever we want for once."

"Whatever we want." The words felt funny rolling off my tongue, but in a good way. "Where would we go?"

He shrugged, his eyes twinkling in the pale pink light that was flowing through the living room window. "Where do you want to go?"

God, the possibilities were endless, yet I couldn't choose one. "I don't know...someplace warm, I guess."

He laughed softly and it was a genuine laugh; the kind of laugh that lit up his bright green eyes; the kind of laugh that made my heart skip a beat. "And we'll fly there, like how normal people travel because we'll have all the time in the world..." He trailed off, his face growing serious. "We'll have all the time in the world to spend together....forever, like we promised."

I would have said something, but I was choking on the rapid thudding of my heart. I looked away at the floor. It sounded like such a nice plan...and what if it actually ended up happening—could it actually happen?

221

I felt his fingers graze across the back of my neck—across my Foreseers' mark—moving downward until they were touching my shoulder blade where my Keeper's mark was tattooed.

My eyelids fluttered. *Oh my God.*

"Gemma," he whispered with so much want.

And suddenly I knew what I wanted. A life I'd never pictured before—a life I never thought I could picture. I jumped up and left Alex sitting on the couch with his mouth hanging open. I barreled up the stairs and burst into my bedroom. I ran over to my dresser and grabbed the mapping ball from out of the top drawer.

Yes, I knew what I wanted more than anything.

I wanted to fix it all, so I could live a normal life with the boy waiting for me downstairs.

Chapter 25

"Should we wake everyone up?" Alex asked when I returned to the living room with the mapping ball glittering in my hand.

I shook my head, my smile way too inappropriate for the situation I was about to put myself into. I knew what I was doing was dangerous, for the clear fact that I didn't know what I was doing. All I could hope was that I would be able to find the vision and change it back to what it was. All I had to do was erase my dad, before he ruined everything.

It sounded so simple, yet it wasn't. I mean, first off, just how many memories was I going to have to sort through before I made it to the right one? Nicholas had said the answer was in my mind, but what did that even mean? And then, there was always the concern that Nicholas had been feeding me a line when he told me all I had to do was erase my father before he recreated the vision.

Here's the thing, though. I had a mom upstairs, branded by the mark of evil; a beautiful vampire friend, who was so sad it made my heart break every time I looked at him; a witch friend who was afraid to show who she really was; and a gorgeous guy sitting next to me who I wanted to lean over and press my lips to his, yet I couldn't.

All this...well, it was enough for me to want to go in there and risk whatever I needed to, so I could fix it. So I could take the pain away from everyone and give them a future without death, loneliness, and despair.

So, I stood in the middle of the living room, opened my hand, and let the Purple Flame ignite. And I had to admit, it made me feel kind of powerful.

The purple glow lit up the worry in Alex's bright eyes, but he didn't say anything. He was letting me go be the Gemma I was supposed to be.

"Don't worry," I told him with a small smile. "This is what I was made to do."

And with those last words, I set the mapping ball in my hand, right into the Purple Flame.

Then, I was gone.

Chapter 26

Actually, no I wasn't. I thought I was, but when I opened my eyes, I was still in the living room, the Purple Flame burning as the glittering mapping ball sparkled in my hand.

"It didn't work." Alex's mouth slipped into a frown.

I frowned too, glowering at the mapping ball. "But, why didn't it work?"

Alex came over and examined the mapping ball without touching it. "I don't know...maybe the Purple Flame wasn't what we needed. I mean, you did get the idea from a note left on your bed." He leaned away. "We don't even know who left the note."

Someone who smelt an awful lot like Nicholas, I thought, remembering the smell of flowers that had lingered outside my window after I found the note. But I didn't say anything about this out loud, not wanting to look like a nut job and all.

"Yeah, but, I mean, the Purple Flame existed." I glanced at the flame burning brightly in my hand. "It's got to be used for something."

We stood silently, staring at the flame, trying to put all the pieces of the puzzle together. But the only answer we got was the tick of the clock.

I sighed, removed the mapping ball from my hand, and smothered out the Purple Flame. "Dammit, I thought I had it."

"Maybe that's the problem." Alex dragged his finger across my lip and I found myself growing more frustrated because I was supposed to be fixing everything so I could kiss his lips. "Maybe it's because you're trying too hard...sometimes your power doesn't work when you drain yourself dry."

"Yeah, I guess that could be it."

He quickly brushed his finger across my cheek. The touch was enough to make me shiver...and want more.

"Maybe you should go lie down and try to sleep for a bit, and then try again when you wake up." His voice cracked and I wondered if he felt it too—the want.

"Okay, I will." And then I practically ran upstairs, figuring the sooner I got to sleep, the sooner I could wake up and fix all this. And the sooner Alex and I could have our future.

Okay, so the sleeping thing wasn't working. I was too restless to sleep. I couldn't stop thinking about Alex. The prickle was also going wild, pouring all these weird feelings through me. So, instead of sleeping, I ended up lying

226

in my bed, staring up at the ceiling, trying to decipher the meaning behind these feelings. But it was ending up being as difficult as getting into the mapping ball.

And that's when I heard it. *The voice*—that's what I was calling it.

"The answers to your problems aren't in your ceiling?" it said.

I gave a quick glance from left to right. "Who's there?"

"That's not the question you should be asking." The voice *tsked* me. "You're not focusing on the problem."

I sat up, wondering if I was losing it. "Are you the one who left the note?"

He made an annoying buzzer sound. "Wrong question again."

"Who are you?" I asked, climbing off my bed. "And why does it sound like you're disguising your voice like a game show host?"

"Gemma." The voice sounded so disappointed. "You need to stop focusing on other things and start focusing on saving the world."

"That's kind of what I've been doing," I said, offended. I walked over to my closet and threw it open, expecting to see someone hiding inside, but nope. It was empty.

"Come on, Gemma, ask me the right question."

I shook my head, frustrated that I was now hearing voices while I was awake. But I decided to give it try. "The right question…How can I get into the mapping ball?"

"With the Purple Flame." the voice answered in the same annoying talk-show-host tone that I knew was a disguise.

"I already got the Purple Flame," I told the voice. "It didn't work."

Silence.

I sighed, and mimicking the annoying talk-show-host tone, I asked, "How do I get the Purple Flame to work with the mapping ball?"

"*Ding, ding,* there you go," the voice said with exaggerated cheerfulness.

Oh, my God. This was the weirdest thing ever.

"Now look at your arm," the voice commanded.

I did. "Okay…it looks like an arm—well, except for the ugly olive-green lines tracing my skin." I turned my hand over and looked at the hideous lines Stasha left on my skin when she tried to kill me. "Wait, is that what's doing it?"

Silence.

"Hello?" I called out, trying not to be too loud on the chance that someone might hear me and think I had gone off the deep end.

"You can't restore life with death in your hand," the voice said in a serious tone.

Strangely enough, that actually made sense. "But it's permanent, so how can I make it go away?"

"Go back and ask her to take it away." The voice was fading.

"Are you crazy?" I said, glancing under my bed, wondering if someone was hiding under there. "Stasha will kill me."

There was no one under the bed so I stood up and put my hands on my hips. "Okay, so are you suggesting that I go to the person who tried to kill me and ask her to take her death out of my hand?"

Nothing. No response. No annoying *ding, dings*.

Great. Now what? I sighed. I guess I was going to Stasha's.

I decided it was best not to go alone. I might sound like a coward, but I didn't care. Visiting a girl who had tried to murder me was making me a little bit edgy. I needed backup just in case something bad went down, and I was guessing something would. The best person I could think of to take with me was Laylen because, a) unlike Alex, he had never dated Stasha, therefore his presence would keep any jealous fits of rage to a bare minimum, and, b) Laylen was immortal so Stasha's touch wouldn't kill him.

It was still early as I tiptoed down the hallway to the room that Laylen was sleeping in. Alex was still downstairs; I could hear him moving around as I crept by the stairway. I decided not to tell him I was going, because he would want to come, and like I said, this just didn't seem like a good idea.

I cracked open the door and peeked my head in. "Laylen," I whispered, but all I got in response was a snore.

Great. I hope he's decent.

I slipped inside, shut the door, and flipped on the light. "Laylen."

I scared him—I got that as he jumped out of the bed, arms flying, ready to attack.

He calmed down when he saw it was me. "Gemma, what the heck?"

I pulled an 'I'm-sorry face', but my cheeks heated as I realized he was not decent. He only had on a pair of boxers and I quickly turned around to hide my blushing face.

"I'm sorry." I shook my head at myself. "I should have knocked first."

"It's okay," he said, moving around, hopefully putting on a pair of pants. "But what exactly are you doing?"

I heard the sound of a zipper shutting, but I didn't dare turn around until he gave me the okay. "I need your help with something," I explained, my eyes glued to the door.

The jingling of a belt buckle. "Okay, you can turn around."

I waited a second longer before I turned around and I was relieved to find that he now had pants on, but he was still shirtless and I couldn't help but be dazzled by the sight. I bit at my bottom lip, trying not to stare as he slipped on a black t-shirt, covering up both his Keeper mark cupping his shoulder and his muscles.

"You good?" he asked. "Because you look a little flushed."

"I'm fine," I assured him, but my skin was betraying me.

"That's what you get for barging in on people while they're sleeping," he teased making me blush even more.

Pull yourself together. I cleared my throat, trying to clear out any embarrassment still lingering inside me. "So, yeah, I need your help with something."

He raised his eyebrows at me curiously. "Oh yeah? With what?"

"With paying a visit to Stasha."

His expression fell flat. "I don't think that's such a good idea." He glanced at my olive-green scarred arm. "Considering what happened the last time you went there."

"But I need to," I said. "The Purple Flame won't work unless I do."

"Wait, you got the Purple Flame? When?"

I guess I needed to back up a few steps and tell him what happened.

"So you think the scars on your arms are what's stopping the Purple Flame from working?" he asked after I finished telling him what was going on. Well, minus the details of how I had gotten the information about the scars. I mean, Laylen was understanding and everything, but telling him that a talk-show-host voice told me I needed to visit Stasha…I even thought I sounded crazy.

I nodded. "Yeah, I'm pretty sure."

"But how?" He swept his blue-tipped bangs away from his forehead. "How do you know?"

Crap. "Would you believe me if I said that a little birdie told me?"

He gave me a look like he thought I was insane, but Laylen being Laylen did not press further. "Okay, if that's what you think, then let's go to Stasha's to get the marks removed from your arm." He rubbed his jawline with a thoughtful expression. "But if she tries to kill you again, I might have to use some violence."

"And that's okay with me." I got to my feet and took his hand. "Are you ready?"

"I'm ready," he replied, standing to his feet, towering over me.

I shut my eyes and moments later, we were being swept away.

Chapter 27

The plants. How could I forget about the plants? Yet I did, not remembering until I was standing under them as they hung from the olive-green ceiling of Stasha's living room.

"Careful," I told Laylen, pointing up at the ceiling. "They come alive."

He glanced up at the vines warily. "They do?"

I nodded. "They attacked me the last time I was here."

Laylen pulled a disgusted face at the vines and then we crept through the house to find Stasha. But we found the house empty.

"I don't think she's here," I said, announcing the obvious.

"Good observation," he joked, and I pulled a face at him. "But that just means we can take her by surprise."

I pointed a finger at him. "I like the way you think." But then I grew serious. "You seem better…a little bit anyway with the whole," I pointed at my teeth, "thing."

He flopped down on the living room couch and rested his arms across the top of it. "I am doing a little bit better…but I mean, it's still there." He furrowed his eyebrows. "Did you know Aislin came to me and said she was sorry for everything? It was really weird."

"Really weird," I said, wondering if it had anything to do with the talk we had about Laylen and me being just friends. I roamed around the room, glancing at the photos' hanging on the walls. One photo in particular, resting on the shelf, made me stop in my tracks. It was a picture of Stasha and Alex, smiling as the sunlight sparkled in their hair. I picked up the picture and stared down at it, thinking about Alex's and my "future talk." Would we ever have pictures like this? Ones of smiles and happiness?

I hoped so.

I put the picture back on the shelf and moved along to the next shelf, which had a collection of leaves on it.

"What is her deal with plants?" I muttered. "I mean, I know it's good for her gift but…it's still weird." I glanced up at the ceiling. "And I wonder how she makes them come to—"

"Shhh," Laylen hissed, jumping up from the couch. "I think I hear something."

We stood silent, listening as the sound of footsteps moved toward the door. Laylen and I skittered to the hallway, ducking down, waiting to attack. We heard the jingling of keys and then the door creaked open.

"I don't know why he made me take one of you stupid things," Stasha said, slamming the door. "I mean, it's not like you do any good. And I can't even hear what you're saying."

I tensed up. She was not alone. This was going to make things a little complicated.

"And don't ruin my plants," she snapped. "I need them to keep me alive."

Ah, so that's why she needed the plants. An image of me destroying all her plants popped into my mind, but I shook it away. I needed her alive, otherwise these marks on my arm were here to stay.

"This is ridiculous." Stasha sounded furious and I was starting to wonder who she was having a rude one-sided conversation with. "Do you leak ice or something?"

Laylen's head whipped in my direction and my eyes widened. Did she just say ice?

My heart sped up as the realization that the air had drastically dropped in temperature smacked me in the face. How had I not felt it until now? Usually I could feel their cold from a mile away. Perhaps it had something to do with me being a Keeper now.

"So, do you want to take down Stasha or the Death Walker?" I whispered in Laylen's ear.

He considered this. "I'll take death girl, since you've proven you can handle a Death Walker...besides, her touch won't kill me."

I nodded and he handed me a knife from his pocket.

"We'll have to make it quick, though." I clutched the small knife in my hand. "This thing won't kill it."

Laylen peeked around the corner and then glanced back at me. "Okay, the Death Walker's on the couch." We

235

exchanged a peculiar look. "And Stasha's watering her plants."

I rolled my eyes and held the knife in the perfect attack position. Laylen nodded and raised his hand, counting down on his fingers...three...two...one.

We leapt out form the hallway and took them both by surprise. The Death Walker's eyes lit up. Stasha dropped her pail and water puddled across the floor. The chill of the room immediately froze the water over and ice crackled all over the walls and vines, freezing everything in its place. The Death Walker's yellow eyes lit up with rage beneath the hood of its black cloak. Laylen darted toward Stasha and she picked up a ceramic rose and chucked at him. It hit him in the shoulder and scattered across the floor.

I turned my attention away from them and focused on the death monster, hovering toward me, thirsty to kill. But, like at the castle, I felt in control, knowing I could take the evil ice-machine down. I started to circle it and it followed my movement, circling me back. It's yellow-eyes were locked on me, waiting to attack. I held the knife out in front of me, the sharp point glinting in the light. It was now or never. So, with one quick movement, I lunged forward and stabbed the knife into its chest and then ducked for cover because I knew what was coming—the Chill of Death. Its death breath puffed through the air as its body rocked and swayed, before tipping over and hitting the floor with a loud crash. I whirled around, relieved to see that Laylen had gotten Stasha pinned up against the wall.

She looked furious, her blue eyes glaring ferociously at Laylen. "You're messing up my hair," she whined.

I hopped over the Death Walker and moved over beside Laylen.

Stasha's eyes instantly narrowed on me. "Well, well, look who was stupid enough to come back." She smirked. "What? Was my trying to kill you not enough of a warning that you should never be around me?"

"You, know, it really doesn't seem like you're in much of a position to be such a…"

"Bitch," Laylen finished for me.

"Exactly."

Stasha shot me a dirty look, but winced as Laylen pushed her harder against the wall.

"Fine, what do you want?" she asked.

I held up my olive-green scarred arm. "I want you to take your death out of my arm."

She shook head. "No way."

Laylen and I looked at each other with devious expressions on our faces.

"What do you think we should do?" he asked me.

I glanced back at the unconscious Death Walker slumped on the floor and pointed at the knife sticking out of its chest. "Well, we could always use that on her."

Stasha let out a loud snort. "This is hilarious. I mean, here you are a vampire who won't feed. Oooh, scary. And you." She shot me a malicious look. "You're the pathetic girl who can't feel anything."

"Couldn't," I corrected her. "I'm perfectly capable of feelings now. In fact, I'm pretty sure I have enough anger in me right now that I might just have to…" The sight of Laylen's fangs descending made me trail off.

Stasha's eyes widened as he moved his fangs toward her neck.

"I'm not the same vampire you once knew, Stasha," Laylen hissed through his fangs and I shuddered. "I'm perfectly capable of feeding now."

Stasha was terrified and I had to say that the look was not a good one for her.

"Fine. I'll remove my death from your hand," she gritted through her teeth. "But you two are lucky that that stupid monster's ice froze over my plants, otherwise this would have gone down differently."

"And if you try to kill her instead of removing the death, I'll drain you of all you blood, got it?" Laylen said, his fangs still pointing sharply from his mouth.

"Got it," Stasha said with attitude.

Laylen slightly loosened his grip so Stasha could slip off her gloves.

"Why do you even have one of those things in your house?" Laylen asked, nodding his head at the Death Walker.

"Why not?" Stasha pulled off her glove and tossed it on the floor. "Give me your arm," she told me.

238

Hesitantly, I reached my scarred arm out to her, holding my breath as she wrapped her deathly fingers around my wrist. Within seconds, the olive-green lines were fading away, until my skin was back to its normal paleness. I let out a breath as she moved her hand away, but then gasped as I caught sight of something on her wrist.

A black triangle pointing around a red symbol.

Laylen followed my gaze and his bright blue eyes went wide. "Where did you get that?" he asked.

Stasha glanced down at her marked wrist. "What? This? I've always had it."

Laylen shook his head. "No, you haven't."

"Yes, I have," she said in a low, condescending tone. "I've had it since the day I was born."

"Alex would have never dated you if you had it," I said, but then I questioned my own words.

Laylen was questioning them too, but before any more words could be exchanged, the Death Walker suddenly leapt to its feet and let out a loud shriek.

"Time to go," I said quickly and reached for Laylen's hand.

He knocked Stasha to the floor before taking it. And as the Death Walker charged at us, its yellow eyes glowing, ready to devour, I blinked us away, back to the house.

Chapter 28

"I don't even know what to think," Laylen said.

He was sitting on my bed, his fangs put back where they belonged, and his bright blue eyes wide as we tried to figure out what to do with the whole Stasha-being-marked-with-evil situation. I mean, it wasn't like I hadn't already thought she was evil, but the mark being there...it just shouldn't have been there. And yet it was and it was popping up all over. The thing that was really getting at me, though, was that Stasha said she had had the mark since she was born. So did Alex know about it? If he did, then, I felt like we were back to where we started; back to where I thought he was a liar.

"We should at least give him the benefit of the doubt," I said, fiddling with a loose string on my purple comforter. "See how he reacts when we tell him."

Laylen nodded. "Yeah, I think that's a good idea." He met my eyes with a concerned look on his face. "You're okay, right?"

I glanced down at where the lines once traced my arm. "Yeah, I don't think she did anything to me besides remove her death."

240

He shook his head. "No, not with that. I mean, with the Alex thing. I know how far you two have come so you can trust him."

I pressed my lips together. "Like I said, we should go talk to him—give him the benefit of the doubt, before we start accusing him of anything."

"Alright then." Laylen got to his feet and I followed.

"Are you okay?" I asked him as we headed down the stairs. I didn't have to explain what I meant—was he okay with bringing out his fangs.

"I'm good. In fact, it was kind of nice to bring them out for a good cause."

"Well, if it does start to bother you," I started to say.

But he threw his arm around my shoulder. "I know. I know. I'll come talk to you first, before bailing."

Alex, Aislin, and Aleesa were in the living room when Laylen and I walked in. Aislin was typing away on the laptop, so determined to figure out why the spell at the cemetery didn't work. Alex was trying to explain to Aleesa what a television was, and how people were not trapped inside it.

"Hey," he said when he caught sight of me in the doorway. His eyes flickered in Laylen's direction and then he said to me, "I thought you were resting so you could try to go in the mapping ball again."

Aleesa let out a giggle at something on the TV.

"I couldn't sleep." I stared at him, my pulse racing as his bright green eyes burned intensely back at me. *Please,*

please, say you didn't know about the mark. I raised my arm, figuring that was the best place to start.

His eyebrows dipped down. "Where'd it go?"

I bit on my bottom lip. "We paid Stasha a little visit."

"What?" His face reddened with anger, but he kept his tone calm. "You paid her a visit?"

"Yeah…I had this hunch that maybe if her death scars weren't on my arm, the Purple Flame might work," I explained.

"Okay…well, I wish you would have said something before you took off," he said, trying his hardest to stay calm. "But since you're without the scars I assume everything went okay."

I shook my head, leaning against the doorway. "Not exactly."

Alex glanced back and forth between Laylen and me. "What do you mean, not exactly?"

I looked at Laylen and then at Aislin, who was suddenly very interested in what we were talking about.

"Can I talk to you alone for a minute?" I asked Alex.

He gave me a funny look, but set the TV remote down and followed me out of the room and into the kitchen.

"So…what's wrong?" he asked, leaning back against the teal cupboards and folding his arms.

I sighed. "Well, when Laylen and I—"

He let out a weird sound that sounding kind of like a snort mixed with a cough.

"What was that?" I asked.

242

He shrugged. "What was what?"

I eyed him suspiciously. "That weird noise you just made…why did you make it?"

He shrugged again, looking a lot like the old "whatever" Alex.

"Hey, don't do that," I said. "Don't shut me out. Just tell me what's wrong."

He stared at me for a moment and then he was moving toward me, stopping just short of running into me.

"My problem is that every time you have a problem, you run off with him." He pointed over his shoulder toward the living room where I knew Laylen was sitting. "It's driving me crazy."

Okay…he was being honest, which was kind of weird. "Well." I took a step back because the sparks were a little overwhelming. "It seemed better to take Laylen with me this time because Stasha can't kill him with her touch, him being immortal and all."

"And that's the only reason?" His bright green eyes glimmered like gems as he waited for me to answer.

"Yeah." I think that was the right answer.

He relaxed and I started to relax until I remembered.

"Wait a minute," I took a step toward him. "I have to ask you something."

He looked confused. "Okay…."

I took a deep breath. "Did you know Stasha has the Mark of Malefiscus?"

His jaw fell. "She doesn't."

243

"Yes, she does. I saw the mark on her wrist, and she told us she's had it since she was born."

"That's not possible. I would know if she had."

I hated that he would know. "So you're saying you didn't know."

"I'm saying there's no way she could have one, unless she got it after we stopped...dating."

I rubbed my hands across my face, feeling the stress. "I guess she could have been lying about that part, but I don't know why."

"Or do you think I'm lying?" he questioned with an arch of his eyebrow.

I hesitated. "I don't think you're lying."

He shook his head. "Now who's lying?"

I started to protest, but he was stepping for me, backing me up until my back pressed into the counter.

"You don't believe me, do you?" he asked.

I held his gaze. "If you tell me you didn't know, then I'll believe you."

He placed his hands on the counter, so I was trapped between his arms. Then he leaned in, his face merely inches away from me. "I didn't know she had the mark."

He was telling the truth—I could see it in his eyes. But I waited a second or two, before confessing this, because...well, because I was kind of enjoying being trapped between his arms.

"Okay, I believe you," I finally said, and he waited a second or two before he stepped back and freed me from

244

his arms. I shook off the sparks. "So, why do you think she's marked then? And why would she have a Death Walker at her house?"

He gaped at me. "What?"

"Oh, did I forget to mention that?" I asked, and he nodded with an astonished look on his face. "Well, she had one there."

Alex ran his fingers through his hair. "This just doesn't make any sense. I mean, why the sudden abundance of marks? They were supposed to be nonexistent."

"Do you think your dad's going around, marking everyone, like he did with Nicholas and some of the Keepers?" I asked.

"He could be." He shrugged. "I guess, but didn't that witch Medea say she had it since she was born and that there were others?"

"I know….it's so weird," I mumbled. "Like something's changed."

We looked at each other, perplexed.

"Well, maybe it's time for you to put everything back to what it was." Alex pointed at my arm. "You think that thing's ready to go?"

I raised my arm up, examining it. "Let's find out."

I went and grabbed the mapping ball, and moments later I was standing in the kitchen with the Purple Flame burning vibrantly in my hand. Alex stood over by the counter, arms folded as he watched me with an uneasy look on his face.

I took a deep breath, crossed my fingers that it would work—it had to work—and set the glittering mapping ball into my hand.

Then, I was gone.

Chapter 29

It was too dark—I had to be dead. I panicked, thinking how completely and one hundred percent stupid it was for me to believe that a note left on my bed and a talk-show-host voice would give me the correct way to get inside the mapping ball. Go find the Purple Flame, go erase the death marks, what had I been thinking?

But then, I realized that my eyes were just closed, and when I opened them up, I was dazzled by the most beautiful sight. And I'm not talking about Alex. Stars. Yes, stars, sparkling beneath my feet like diamonds.

"It's beautiful," I whispered in amazement. But my amazement quickly vanished as I realized I had no idea what I was doing.

I walked across the stars, my heart sinking in despair. "What am I supposed to do?"

As if answering me, one of the stars, right in front of my feet flickered. I jumped back as it lit up against the darkness like a movie screen. On the screen was a man probably about twenty years old with dark brown hair and violet eyes—my dad. He was talking to an older woman with long red hair, wearing a perfectly pressed tan dress...it was Sophia.

"Well, I don't see how that would be possible," Sophia said to my father as they walked up the hill toward the Keeper's castle. "Jocelyn's too busy with things. She's supposed to be taking her Keeper's test soon."

"I understand your concern." My dad tried to dazzle her with a charming smile. "But I promise you, I won't keep her out that long."

Sophia, unaffected by my dad's charm, fixed him with a stern gaze—a gaze I have seen many times. "Well, I'll have to think about it and discuss it with her father."

My father smiled, his violet eyes shining like jewels in the sunlight. "That's all I'm asking."

Sophia gave him a nod and walked away, leaving him on the hill. My father picked up a rock and threw it into the lake, making the dark blue water ripple. He looked happy, not like someone who had been—or would be—the cause of the world ending in ice and death.

The scene dulled away and dropped back into the star. Not the vision I was looking for, but it was interesting to see my dad, just a normal guy, wanting to ask my mom out.

Another star lit up, illuminating the darkness with another screen. My father, still twenty-something years old, sat next to a woman with dark brown hair and bright blue irises—my mom. They were in what looked like the corner of a library, huddled together, a stack of books piled at their feet.

"I still don't understand why you have to help him," my mother said to my father in a low voice.

My father took her hands in his. "Everything will be okay. I'll help Stephan and he assured me that we can be together if I do; that your parents won't have any problems with us wanting to get married."

My mother looked like she wanted to say something, but couldn't. "Julian, please don't do this."

"It'll be alright." My dad held her face in his hands. "Stephan just needs my help with something and then this will all be over."

She swallowed hard, and again she looked like she wanted to say something. "But, help with what? Has he even told you?"

He shook his head. "He hasn't, but I'm sure it'll be fine."

My mother scratched at her wrist, right where the Mark of Malefiscus marked her skin. But her long-sleeved white shirt covered it up and I wondered if my father knew it was there. She kept scratching and scratching at it like she was trying to scratch it away.

"Please, don't go, Julian," she begged "I'm begging you not to."

My father pressed his lips together and leaned in to kiss her. "I have to, otherwise, I'll never have this."

I let out a shaky breath as the picture faded back into the star. They seemed so normal and in love, not evil, not marked with the Mark of Malefiscus, not about to end the world.

I moved on to the next star and waited for it to light up. But when the screen blazed across the blackness, my body tensed up. Stephan, dressed all in black, sitting at a long mahogany table. Across from him, was my dad. His arms were resting on the table, the sleeves of his dark blue shirt rolled up revealing that his arms and wrists were free of marks.

"I have to say, Julian, I'm surprised you showed up." Stephan's grin was as evil as ever. "Jocelyn must mean a lot to you."

My dad shifted in the chair uneasily. "Is it true you can create marks? Can you really mark me as a Keeper?"

That's what he wanted. He wanted Stephan to make him a Keeper. He hadn't mentioned this to my mom. Why had he kept it a secret?

"Hmmm..." Stephan traced his finger across the scar on his face. "Is it true there's a way for a Foreseer to change a vision?"

My dad's face fell. ""I—I don't think so."

Stephan leaned toward my father, his fingernails digging into the wood as he pressed his hands firmly into the table. "You know what I hate more than anything, Julian? People who lie. I can't stand liars."

250

And that coming from the mouth of the biggest one I've ever met.

"I'm not lying, sir," my dad said with an uneasiness that gave away his lie.

Something flashed in Stephan's dark eyes that made me cringe. "I understand there are rules Foreseers have that forbid you to tell me what I ask." He pushed back from the chair and walked around to the other side of the table, towering above my father. "Give me your arm, Julian."

"What?" My father gaped up at Stephan. "Why do you need my arm?"

"Give. Me. Your. Arm," Stephan repeated in a calm but firm tone.

My dad let out a loud breath and held out his arm. Stephan pulled a knife from his pocket and with one swift movement, stabbed it into my father's arm. "*Vos es venalicium.*"

My dad let out a cry of pain, his fingers moving for the knife. But it was too late; a mark had already burned into his wrist. Blood seeped out of his pale skin and dripped onto the stone floor. My dad pressed his hand down on the wound. "Why did you...I don't understand," he stammered.

Stephan tossed the knife onto the table, the blade stained red with my father's blood. "Now you have no choice but to help me."

My father clenched his jaw in pain, lifted his blood soaked hand away from his arm and gasped.

So did I.

A black triangle tracing a red symbol marked his wrist. The Mark of Malefiscus.

"But you said you would give me the Keeper's mark." My father raised his marked wrist. "What is this?"

Stephan grinned wickedly. "Oh, you'll soon find out."

The light faded away into the star, and I sank to the blackened ground, sitting on the stars, trying to keep it together. My mother lied. My father didn't want power. He wanted to be with her. He thought he was becoming a Keeper. Why would my mom lie about this? Or did she not know the truth? Was the only story she knew from Stephan?

I shook my head. The man had ruined way too many lives. I stood up, filled with the determination to fix it. But there were so many stars…it could take forever. I needed a way to figure out which one held the right memory.

Think, Gemma, think.

I sorted through my memories, trying to think of something—anything—that was mentioned that might help. Both Nicholas and my dad had said something about my mind having the answers, but right now, my mind seemed as blank as a sheet of paper.

I gazed at all the stars…if I could just see which one I…needed. Oh my word. I jumped to my feet and focused on not seeing the stars, but seeing *the* star; the one that

252

held the memory of my dad changing the vision. The stars began to sparkle as if they were playing a silent melody of color and light. Then, suddenly, a silver cloud rose up from the ground. I jumped back as it slithered across the stars like a magical snake, heading into the darkness.

Was that my answer?

I chased after it as it weaved around stars, until it finally came to a stop above one; a purple one that shined brighter than all the other stars near it. The magical snake swooped up into the air and swan-dived down into the star. I held my breath, waiting for the screen to light up, but there was nothing. No light. No movie clip.

I leaned over the star, trying to see what was inside it. But the only thing I could see was a faint purple light emitting from the center of it. Hesitantly, I touched my finger to the star.

Energy jolted through my body, and the ground shook like an earthquake.

I let out a scream as the floor beneath me collapsed.

Chapter 30

I was falling through darkness lit up by shimmering stars, tumbling toward the unknown. It seemed like I fell forever, until finally my feet landed lightly on the ground, as if someone had caught me and slowed me down, which was a good thing since I probably would have broken a few bones with how fast I was falling.

Although, I wasn't sure, I was guessing this was it. This was *the* one; the memory that I needed.

I was standing with my back to Keeper's grey stone castle, the lake stretched out before me. It looked like winter-time; the trees crisped with snow, the water was a sheet of sparkling pale blue ice, the sky nothing more than a cloud of grey. However, I wasn't going to assume that it was winter. The snow and ice could be coming from a group of nearby Death Walkers. Or maybe this was the end-of-the-world vision my dad recreated. I suddenly realized I had no idea what was going on. What was I supposed to do? How was I supposed to find out if this was the right memory?

Then, I saw him, my dad, walking down the ice-covered hill, heading for the lake. He was the younger version of my dad, like the one I saw in the other memories. But he wore the same silver robe I saw him wearing in the Room of Forbidden. His face was solemn, his violet eyes fixated on the lake. He did not see me as he walked by me, and I carefully followed after him.

"Where is it?" he muttered to himself as he came to a stop at the edge of the lake.

As if on cue, I saw them, creeping out from the tall icicled trees that encircled the lake. Death Walkers. Their black cloaks dragged across the snowy ground and the glow of their yellow eyes reflected across the icy lake.

I shivered as they marched toward us, hoping they couldn't see me. The ground shook with the beat of their footsteps and I heard my dad's breath catch as a man appeared at the edge of the trees, not too far off from where we stood.

Stephan.

He was wearing a black cloak with the hood pulled over his head, but the scar grazing his left cheek let me know it was him. His dark eyes seemed to darken everything around us, along with the pleased look on his face. He motioned for someone to follow him, and another man, much shorter than Stephan, wearing a long, black cloak, stepped out of the forest.

Demetrius.

"There it is," my dad muttered from beside me, staring not at Demetrius and Stephan or at the murderous

Death Walkers marching at us, but at something else; something at the shoreline of the frozen lake.

I squinted my eyes. What was he looking at? There was something there...a blur of colors and shapes. I focused harder and the colors and shapes started to shift and take the form of two figures hugging, clutching onto one another for dear life.

"Oh, my God." My heart stopped.

Alex and I hugging by the lake.

I shook my head, my breath puffing out erratically. Was this what my father created or erased?

The Death Walkers, Stephan, and Demetrius headed for us, the ice rumbling and the snow falling from the trees as the world shook beneath the pounding of their footsteps. I watched as Alex brushed my hair from my face.

"It'll be okay," he whispered softly.

"How do you know?" I whispered back, tears streaming from my eyes.

"Because I do," he replied, brushing another strand of my hair back and tucking it behind my ear. Then he kissed me with so much passion that, even from where I was standing, I could feel the air electrify. He kept kissing and kissing me as the electricity intensified, until finally he pulled me against him and I buried my head into his chest as I clutched onto him for dear life. A bright light orbed around us, suffocating the air as it burned brighter and brighter—as it burned everything.

I shielded my eyes, searching the light, trying to see what was happening. I had never gotten past this part in my dreams, but I think deep down I knew what the light meant. It was why I kept seeing nothing but light at the end of my dreams and my visions. It was the same reason why, when Alex had looked in the future mirror, he only saw light.

"So this is what happens right before the portal is about to open...they stop it from happening, by sacrificing their own lives?" my father whispered under his breath as the light dimmed away. He shook his head. "I'm so sorry."

I gasped at the sight of what remained. The sun shined brightly from the sky and the snow had melted. The lake was no longer blanketed by ice, and it no longer carried the march of hundreds and hundreds of Death Walkers: they had all vanished.

Stephan and Demetrius were nothing more than a pile of ash scattered across the grassy ground. Everything had been burned away with the light, including Alex and I. Our bodies were sprawled on the grass, our fingers intertwined as we lay side by side, our eyes sealed shut, no longer breathing.

Tears streamed down my cheeks as my father stepped toward Alex and me, and reached a hand out, preparing to erase us.

"This is what you erased," I whispered through my tears. This is what I had to put back. I had to let this happen. Let Alex and me die.

257

My heart raced in my chest, knowing what I had to do, knowing I had to erase my father before he created a different future; a future where Stephan would win and the world would die a horrible death. But how could I do it? It would basically be like I was killing Alex and myself. That beautiful little talk we had about our future...we didn't even have a future. How could I place my hand on my father and erase him, when I would be erasing Alex and me right along with him?

I cried harder and harder. "I can't do this. I can't do this."

But as my father's hand hovered only an inch away from Alex and I, I knew. I had to.

Sobbing hysterically, I reached a trembling hand toward my father, wondering what he was about to create. Would Alex and I have lived?

"I'm so sorry," I whispered, and then I placed my hand on his shoulder. Just like on the beach, I watched my father vanish into nothing, flickering out like a bad TV reception.

Then, I sank to the ground and cried and cried until all the energy drained out of me and I blacked out.

Chapter 31

When I woke up, I was back out the house. But I didn't open my eyes.

I just couldn't do it. I couldn't face him. I just couldn't. So, I lay there on the sofa, with my eyes shut, pretending I was passed out, while Aislin, Laylen, and Alex sat around discussing what they should do about my unconscious state.

"She's still breathing," Laylen said, worry lacing his tone.

I hated to hear him worry. I knew I should open my eyes so they all knew I was okay, but with that would also come the explaining of what happened. I would have to tell Alex that he and I were going to die in the near future. That what I had changed back was us dying.

"Yeah, she's breathing," Alex said in a panicked tone. "But what if she doesn't wake up? She's been like this for over an hour. And we don't know anything about the mapping ball or how it works...I shouldn't have let her do it."

An hour. Had I been lying here that long?

"I'm sure she'll wake up," Aislin said optimistically, but it was a fake optimism—she was worried along with everyone else.

"Are you?" Alex snapped. "Because the last time I checked, you weren't a Foreseer and couldn't see into the future."

The future. Don't cry, Gemma. Don't cry.

"Alex, calm down, okay," Laylen said. "I'm sure she'll be okay. This stuff happens a lot to her and she always ends up okay."

A pause, and then I felt him beside me.

"Gemma." Alex's electric breath feathered against my ear. "Wake up please."

His voice ripped at my heart, and I couldn't do it anymore. I opened my eyes and Alex leaned back as I sat up.

"Oh, thank God." Aislin pressed her hand to her heart. "You're okay?"

I nodded, unable to look Alex in the eye.

"So, what happened?" Alex asked, watching me intensely with his bright green eyes. "Were you able to do it?"

I pressed my lips together and stared down at my shoes. I really needed to get some new ones. These ones were starting to get worn out.

Alex placed his hand on my chin and turned my head toward him. "What's wrong? Were you not able to do it?"

I swallowed hard. "No, I did it. I changed the vision back to what it originally was."

260

Excitement filled the air.

Alex smiled, his eyes lighting up more than I had ever seen them, and in a minute, when I told him what would happen, it was going to disappear again. "So everything's good. The world's not going to end." He leaned in for a kiss because he thought he could.

I turned my head away.

"What's wrong?" he asked.

I pressed my lips together and squeezed my eyes shut, wishing the pain would go away. "We still can't be together."

Silence choked the room.

"What do you mean?" he asked.

I took a deep breath and looked over at Aislin and Laylen. "Can you two give us a second? I need to talk to Alex alone."

Aislin gave me a weird look. I had to look away at the hurt expression on Laylen's face. I knew what he was thinking: he and I didn't keep secrets from each other. I was planning on telling him, but I think I needed to tell Alex first.

I waited until they both left the room. I waited until the silence almost drove me mad. I waited for as long as I could.

"You and I can't be together because..." My voice shook and I choked back the tears. "Because that's how we save the world. We're together, you and I kill the star...and we...die along with it."

261

The light slipped out of his bright green eyes, just like I thought it would. "That's what is really supposed to happen?" His voice was flat and unemotional. "That was the original vision?"

I nodded, tears soaking my cheeks. "That's what's going to happen."

Silence ticked by. With every tick of the clock, I felt myself closing in on my end, and I was dragging Alex along with me.

Suddenly, Alex jumped to his feet. "I can't..." He stormed out of the room and a second later I heard the front door slam shut.

Aislin and Laylen appeared in the doorway.

"What happened?" Aislin asked, glancing at the front door.

I looked at both of them, standing there, worried without even knowing what was going on. So I took a deep breath and told them what happened—what would happen.

Right away, Aislin took off after Alex. Laylen stood frozen in the doorway, his arms folded, his bright blue eyes locked on me like he was afraid that if he looked away I might disappear.

"Are you okay?" I finally asked him.

His eyebrows furrowed down. "*You're* asking *me* if I'm okay?"

I shrugged, sinking back into the couch. "I worry about you."

He shook his head, astounded by the idea, and sat down on the couch beside me. "So that's how it's going to happen?"

I nodded, staring down at the floor. "That's how it's going to happen."

A pause and then he slipped his arm around my shoulder. "Maybe we could fix it...I don't know...do something."

I shook my head. "No, there's nothing we can do. Everything is back to the way it was supposed to be."

Laylen pulled me against him, and I buried my head into his chest. He let my cry. He let my tears soak his black t-shirt. He stayed silent the whole time.

And that was what I needed for the moment.

After I bawled my eyes out, I asked Laylen to please forgive Aislin because he needed someone. He agreed and then I made a promise to myself that when Aislin returned I would make sure that she kept an eye on Laylen. Even though they both would live, Laylen would still be a vampire, and I knew he would struggle with it. He needed someone to help him, and I could not bear to think that after I was gone, he would have no one.

He would have someone.

I would make sure of that.

It was still light outside, but I went upstairs to take a nap. I was exhausted, both emotionally and mentally. I also wanted to sleep, hoping that I could temporarily leave some of the pain behind.

When I shut my bedroom door I heard my mom yell my name from the next room, but I didn't want to talk to her yet. I would, though, once I pulled myself together.

I clicked on my computer and scanned through my songs, finally deciding on Blink 182's "All of This."

"Take me away," I whispered to the lyrics.

And they did.

Light. Light everywhere.

Alex and I holding onto one another, the lake melting before us.

"Everything will be okay," Alex whispered in my ear. "I promise it will."

Light all around me and I could feel myself slipping away, fading away with the star; fading away with Alex.

Ash covered the ground, the snow lifted away.

"It will be okay."

I woke up, my eyes so swollen they would barely open. So I just lied there on my bed, trying to figure out what time it was. But then I realized how electric my skin felt and my eyes shot open. I lurched back, nearly falling out of bed as a pair of bright green eyes stared at me.

Alex caught my arm and pulled me back on the bed. "Sorry...I was just..."

"Watching me sleep," I finished for him.

"It's not as creepy as it sounds," he said, still holding onto my arm.

"No, it's pretty creepy," I tried to joke, but the tone of my voice cracked.

"You don't have to do that." He released my arm. "You don't have to fake that everything's alright."

"Don't I?" I questioned.

He shook his head. "You don't. Not with me."

Music still flowed from the speakers. I had set it on repeat, so the same song still played softly in the background.

"So how does it happen?" he asked, rolling onto his back and staring up at the ceiling.

I rolled onto my back as well and let out a loud breath. "Do you really want to know?"

"I do."

So I told him, making it sound as lovely and poetic as one can make a death sound.

"It doesn't sound that bad," he said, after I finished.

"I guess not." And deep down, I know it wasn't. Being with Alex, while we died...it could have been a lot worse. But it still didn't mean I had come to terms with it. I didn't want to die. I didn't want Alex to die. I wanted us to be together, for real, not just when we were reaching our end.

Alex turned his head toward me, this strange look on his face as he stared at me. "Will you come somewhere with me?"

"I don't know..." I was hesitant, even though I wanted to.

Just because I knew when we would die, didn't mean we could just run around together. We had to wait until all the Death Walkers gathered, until Demetrius and Stephan were there, until we could burn away the bad all in one shot, right as the portal was about to open.

"I promise things won't get too heated," he said as if he read my mind. "I'll even promise to keep my hands to myself."

I couldn't help but give a soft laugh.

"And if the electricity starts to fade, we'll leave, okay?" he promised.

I swallowed hard, thinking of the light that would fade everything away. "So you felt it too? Back when we were at your house?"

He nodded. "I did—I felt it."

I took a deep breath, my heart aching inside my chest. "Okay, where do you want to go?"

He gave a small smile. "To our little hideout where we made the Blood Promise to be together forever."

I nodded. "Alright, I can take us there."

And I did, trying not to think about the fact that our forever wasn't going to be for very long.

Chapter 32

I used my Foreseer power to takes us to the outskirts of the castle, right in the center of the forest, in front of the bush blooming with violet flowers that hid the entrance to our old childhood hideout.

I didn't ask why Alex wanted to go, but I could feel that being here was important to him. So I followed him up the side of the hill, he helped me over the bush, and I climbed down the ladder, into the dark hideout.

Alex climbed down after me and I stood in the darkness until a candle was lit. The light radiated around the tiny room made of dirt, and we both sat down on the floor with our backs pressed up against the wall, side by side, letting the silence wrap around us. I thought maybe this was what he wanted, to remember the memories the place held, memories which I could still not remember, except for one. A promise made, between Alex and me, a promise to be together forever.

Forum.

"You know, I never stopped thinking about you," he said, looking ahead at the wall. "After you left."

I didn't say anything. I wanted to. I wanted to tell him that I never stopped thinking about him either, but that wouldn't be true. I hadn't thought about him, because I couldn't remember him—I couldn't remember much of anything.

"And then when I first saw you again." He met my eyes. "That day at school…I had so much trouble shutting my emotions off that day." This strange look passed over his face as if he were remembering that day. "All that time spent learning how to shut them off, and one look at these," he brushed the tip of his finger at the corner of my eye, "and everything I learned was momentarily gone."

That I could remember; how the first day I saw him at school, I was magnetized toward him. I felt things that day I had never felt before, and I wondered if somehow, in the back of my mind, I knew who he was; I remembered the Blood Promise, I remembered he was my forever.

"I want to do something," Alex said, turning to face me. "I want to make another Blood Promise."

"A Blood Promise." I raised my eyebrows curiously at him. "What kind of a Blood Promise."

"One that will help us through this." He took a deep breath and slipped a knife out of the pocket of his jeans. "One that will make the impossible possible."

I didn't understand, but he had this look on his face, begging me to promise, begging me to understand, begging me to trust him.

So I nodded. "Alright, let's make a promise." I held out my hand, the one marked with the scar of an older Blood Promise made a very long time ago.

He took a deep breath as he flipped the blade open. Then he cut his hand, and holding my gaze, carefully cut mine.

He pushed our hands together. *"EGO spondeo vos ero totus vox,"* The words poured out of him with a deeper meaning than I could grasp. His bright green eyes were on me, only me and nothing else. *"EGO spondeo EGO mos operor quisquis capit ut servo vos."*

I waited for him to tell me what he needed me to say, but he dropped his hand and put his knife back into his pocket.

"That was a one-sided promise," I said, clutching my hand shut to stop the bleeding.

"It was a one-sided promise that needed to be made." He stood to his feet and helped me to mine.

"But that doesn't seem fair," I said with a frown. "I didn't promise you anything back."

"Trust me," he said. "I got everything I needed."

I could see in his eyes that he did, that whatever he needed from that promise, he got. There seemed to be less heaviness in his eyes because of it.

"We should go back," he said, still holding onto my hand. "If we're gone for too long, everyone will worry that we're *gone* gone."

"If that's what you want." I shut my eyes. "Then let's go back."

Chapter 33

When we returned back to the house, I went up to talk to my mom, figuring it was time to explain to her what was going on. She was awake when I entered the room and she had this look on her face, like she knew I was about to tell her something terrible.

I sat down on the floor in front of her, my heart knocking in my chest as I stared at her for what probably felt like an eternity.

"I saw what happened," I finally told her. "Dad didn't want to be like Stephan. Stephan marked him with the Mark of Malefiscus."

Her expression fell into horror. "W-what?"

"He's not evil," I said, hugging my knees against my chest. "He had to do it—he had to change the vision."

Her blue eyes were huge as she sat there, taking in what I said. "He didn't want the mark?"

I shook my head. "No, he just wanted to be with you."

She swallowed hard and it looked like this invisible burden had been lifted from her shoulders, like she had been suffering in silence for years at the thought that my dad wanted to be evil.

"I changed it back," I told her. "The vision he changed to end the world, I changed it back."

She looked surprised and the chains jingled as she shifted her legs in front of her. "You fixed it."

I plucked at the loose strands of carpet. "I fixed it."

"So, the world doesn't end then?" she asked.

I nodded, not looking at her. "The world doesn't end."

A pause.

"Gemma, what's wrong? I can tell something's bothering you."

Suddenly, I lost it. I started bawling hysterical sobs, and I moved toward my mom and, ignoring the fact that she was chained to the wall because she was marked with the Mark of Malefiscus, I hugged her.

She put her hands around me and gave me what I needed. A loving mother.

And that's how we stayed until the sun set behind the mountains, until the room grew so dark I had to pull away from her so I could get up and turn on the light and finally explain to her why I was crying.

"So that's what he erased?" She struggled to keep control of her voice. "He erased your death."

"And created the world's death in its place," I said, nodding. "I think, either way, I probably would have ended up dying, but this way it is just Alex and me that do. And we take Stephan and all the Death Walkers down with us." I forced a smile. "Which is a good thing, right?"

She gave me this look, this stern you-listen-here-missy kind of look. "You listen to me, Gemma Lucas, you are not going to give up that easily."

"I—I'm not giving up," I stammered, thrown off by her words. "It's what happens. I can't do anything about it."

She shook her head. "There are always loopholes, Gemma."

"You always say that," I said, frustrated. "But I don't know what it means. How are there loopholes? It was a vision—the only loopholes are to do what dad did and try to change it to something else, and all that will get me is a one-way ticket to being trapped in my own mind forever."

"There are always loopholes, Gemma," she repeated, taking me by the shoulders and looking me straight in the eye. "Think about it. Your father took you into the Room of Forbidden, where no one's supposed to enter. You got me out of The Underworld, which isn't supposed to be possible. Your soul is reconnected, which was never supposed to happen. All those things were caused by loopholes." She paused. "Just because you saw your death, doesn't mean you have to die...I'm not saying that what you saw won't happen, but that you need to find your loophole through your death...make it so you survive after the star's power fades away."

I took in her words, unsure whether or not to believe them. Yes, all those things could be caused by loopholes, but a loophole in a vision was different. Visions were seeing things that were going to happen.

"I don't know Mom..." I gave her a doubtful look.

"Do not give up." Her tone was firm—demanding. "I want you to go into your room and read through that Foreseers' book—find your loophole. Promise me, Gemma. Promise me you won't give up."

"Okay, okay, I promise," I said because I didn't have another choice, not with the desperate look on her face; the look that I assume almost every mother would give to their daughter if they were put in our situation.

And so, like almost every daughter, I got to my feet, obeying my mother, to try to find my loophole.

Reading the Foreseers' book was hurting my brain, and I was only about three-quarters of the way through it. Finally, I let out a sigh and set the book aside. I needed a quicker way to read through all this information and I found myself wondering if Aislin knew a spell that could give me a speed reading ability or something.

But then another idea occurred to me; an idea which I had to sit on for a while before I talked myself into doing it.

I *needed* a loophole.

I shut my eyes and let my brain focus on seeing a loophole. I wasn't sure if what I was doing was right, but I had to try. I had to try and find a way for Alex and me to have our forever.

I just had to.

But as I tried to push my brain beyond the boundaries of seeing something that probably wasn't supposed to be seen, I felt an explosion from inside my skull, like my brain had burst.

My eyes shot open.

I saw spots.

Then I tumbled off the bed and blacked out.

Chapter 34

"You can't cheat your way there," a voice said.

My eyelids fluttered open, and the first thing I saw were shoes. A pair of black shoes that shined in the light that flowed around them.

"If you want to find out the answer," the voice said. "You have to search for it on your own."

I rolled over on my back and looked up at my father, towering above me. "Am I in your head again?" I asked.

He smiled a gentle smile and helped me to my feet. "So you discovered where I am, then?"

I nodded, glancing around, noticing we weren't in the same place as we were before. We were on a beach. The ocean's waves crashed toward us and the bright light was the sun shining from the clear blue sky.

"Where are we?" I asked, getting to my feet.

"We are wherever I need us to be," he said, heading down the shore.

I followed him. "But I thought you were in the Room of Forbidden....I thought you were stuck in your own head."

His violet eyes shone brightly in the sun as he looked at me. "I am, but I do get bored sometimes and changing the scenery helps pass the time."

"Okay...but I don't get something....how come the Foreseers put you in here? Why didn't you just tell them what happened...that Stephan made you change the vision because he marked you with that?" I pointed at his wrist, which was covered by the sleeve of his robe.

He looked at me solemnly. "It's the downfall of being a Foreseer, Gemma. There are no second chances or room for mistakes."

"But you didn't willingly make the mistake," I argued as the ocean soaked at my feet. "Stephan made you do it."

Silence passed between us as the ocean crashed back and forth and birds cawed in the background.

"You need to stop worrying about me," he said. "You have other problems to deal with at the moment."

I stopped and stared out at the ocean. "Like saving the world....because I already did that."

"I know you did, but that is not what I'm talking about."

I shielded my eyes from the sun. "Then what are you talking about?"

"What you're in store for." He gazed out at the ocean. "What waits for you in the near future."

"I know what it is," I told him. "I know that I die."

"You're still not getting it," he said, sounding frustrated. "You need to push that aside, otherwise you will never be able to save the world."

I dropped my hand and turned my head toward him. "But I already did that."

"Not quite." He reached into the pocket of his silver robe and pulled out a ring trimmed with violet gems. Then, he took my hand and set the ring in it.

"What is it?" I asked, gazing down at the ring, shimmering in the sunlight.

"That I cannot tell you."

I frowned. "Why do you always say that? How can you give me things like this," I held up the ring, "and the mapping ball, but you can't tell me how to use them? And how do you even have these things, if we're inside your head?"

He gave me an understanding smile. "This is my loophole, Gemma. I'm able to give you these things, because we are in my head and not in the real world. What I do in here does not matter out there. But I cannot tell you how to use them, because that would be interfering with what you need to do out in the real world. You have to figure out the answers for yourself and pave the world with your memories."

I stared at the ring in the palm of my hand. "I still don't get it."

"You will, when the time is right." He shut my hand around the ring. "This is your loophole, Gemma."

278

"My loophole to what? Saving my life or saving the world?" I asked, but the ocean blurred away and the sun began to dim; he was already sending me back.

"And no more trying to cheat, no matter what happens," he called out, his voice sounding far away. "If you're not careful, you'll end up in here."

I frowned, but said no more as I was yanked away, back to my room.

But when I opened my eyes, the boring tan walls of my room did not surround me.

All I could see was light.

Nothing but light.

Chapter 35

"Oh, my God, I'm dead," were the first words that left my mouth.

"You're not dead," someone replied in a soft, purring voice.

I glanced around...I knew that voice. "But you are."

"Am I?" the tricky half-faerie teased. "Are you sure about that?"

I shook my head. "I'm not sure about anything anymore."

I heard the soft thump of his footsteps moving through the light, heading toward me. "Of course, you're not. You never have been." He paused. "In fact, you're the most confused girl I have ever known...always looking for the answers in the wrong places."

"What do you mean?" I asked, and suddenly he was right there, his golden eyes only inches away from me, the smell of flowers and rain smothering me to the point that I gagged.

"How can you be here, if I'm not dead?" I asked.

"I will answer that shortly," he said. "But right now you have to go back." And with that he shoved me backward, his hands searing hot against my shoulders.

I let out a scream as darkness suffocated me.

My eyes flew open and I shot upright, gasping for air. It took me a minute to realize I was on my bedroom floor, safe and sound from potentially dead faeries.

What kind of detour was that? One minute I was talking to my father, and the next thing I know I'm being shoved down by Nicholas.

I got to my feet, the ring that my father gave me clutched tightly in my hand. What was I supposed to do next? The only thing I could do, really. And that was to go inform everyone that the mystery was not yet solved.

"Why does he keep giving you things without an explanation of what they are?" Alex asked as he sat on the couch, twirling the ring in his fingers.

I shrugged. "I don't know...he said it was because I had to figure things out on my own...and pave the world with my memories, whatever that means."

Alex gave me a knowing look and then exchanged a strange look with Laylen.

"So you think there might be a way that we don't have to die?" Alex asked with a hopeful expression.

I shrugged, not wanting to crush his hope, but not wanting to lie either. "I don't know...everyone keeps talking about loopholes...so maybe."

Alex exchanged another look with Laylen. What was this? I mean, it wasn't like the two of them really liked each other or anything, yet they seemed to be exchanging secrets with their eyes.

"Why do you keep giving each other weird looks like that?" I asked suspiciously.

"Yeah, what are you two up to?" Aislin asked form beside me, and I was glad she was noticing their weird behavior too.

Alex set the ring on the coffee table. "We're not up to anything." He got to his feet. "Laylen and I do, however, have somewhere to be."

"Like where?" I asked at the same time Aislin said, "What?"

Laylen glanced at his watch. "Is it time already?"

Alex nodded and they headed for the door.

"Where are you going?" I called out, rising to my feet.

"Don't worry," Alex said, pausing in the doorway. "We'll be back."

Before I could say anything else, they walked out the front door and shut it behind them. I turned around and gaped at Aislin.

"Do you know what that was about?" I asked, pointing over my shoulder at the front door.

She shook her head, looking genuinely perplexed. "It was weird, though...definitely weird."

I sat back down on the couch and picked up the ring my father gave me. "How is a ring my loophole?"

Aislin took the ring from me and examined it. "I'm not sure...but I think we could start by finding out what kind of ring it is."

"Any ideas on how to do that?"

She shrugged and we both sat there, staring at the violet gemmed ring, wondering what to do next.

"So have you figured out what went wrong with your spell?" I asked, taking the ring from her. *What are you for?*

She shook her head. "It's strange...from everything I read, it should work, and I can feel the power and everything, but when I try to use it, I get nothing."

Without even thinking, I slipped the ring onto my finger.

"Gemma, what are you doing?" Aislin sputtered. "You can't just put something like that on...what if it does something to you?"

We both waited in silence, for something to happen; sparks to fly, me to explode, but nothing happened.

I frowned disappointedly and Aislin let out a sigh.

"Did you ask your mom what it was?" Aislin pointed at the ring on my finger. "The ring, I mean."

I shook my head, leaned back in the sofa, and put my feet up on the coffee table. "Not yet."

We grew silent again. I could hear the wind howling outside, and I wondered if a storm was coming.

Aislin opened the laptop. "I think maybe we could—"

A loud bang cut her off. We both looked at each other and then we were on our feet, moving for the kitchen, where the bang came from.

Bang. Bang. Bang.

We paused at the doorway of the kitchen, too afraid to enter as the banging continued to rattle at the air.

"What is that?" Aislin whispered.

I shook my head. "I don't know…do you have like a weapon or something, just in ca—" I trailed off as smoke whirled across the floor, brushed across my ankles and drifted into the living room.

"Where is that coming from?" Aislin asked as more smoke swept across the floor.

"I don't know." For some reason, though, I thought of the vision I saw, the one where the streets of Afton were filled with fire.

Aislin slipped a knife out of the pocket of her shorts and held it up in front of her. "On the count of three?"

I nodded. "On the count of three…one…two…three."

We both jumped into the kitchen, ready to kick some butt. But no butt kicking was necessary because the smoke was coming from a fire burning in the garbage can outside in the driveway. The back door had been left open and was swinging away against the wind, letting the smoke blow into the house.

Aislin lowered her knife. "Oh, thank God. For a second I thought the house was burning down or something"

But I was not relieved. "Yeah, but who started the fire?"

She shrugged. "I don't know...maybe some kids who were bored?"

"Maybe." But her answer didn't feel right.

We crept over to the door, watching the fire blaze against the night.

Something was wrong.

I could feel it.

The sight of the fire was setting off something inside me and I couldn't stop thinking about the vision I had right after I was bit by the vampire; the chaos in the streets, the fires, Stephan. *You need to prepare yourself*, my father had said.

"Do you have a fire extinguisher?" Aislin asked.

I pointed to the cupboard below the kitchen sink, but my eyes stayed on the fire. "It's under there."

Moments later, Aislin was putting out the fire with a satisfied look rising on her face when she finished. "There, fire problem all taken care of."

I forced a smile as she went back into the house and put the extinguisher back in the cupboard.

"Something's not right," I muttered.

Something definitely wasn't right.

Chapter 36

Aislin and I went back to the living room and Aislin started searching the internet, trying to find more details on her
spell, while I read through the Foreseers' book, trying to
figure out what the ring on my finger was for, even though
I had no idea if it even had anything to do with Foreseers.
But it was hard to concentrate when I couldn't stop thinking about the fire. It felt like it was an omen or
something—a warning that something bad lay ahead for
all of us. But I couldn't figure out how. I had changed the
vision back to what it was. The world was not supposed to
end anymore.

It seemed like hours ticked by before I heard the front
door open and Alex and Laylen walked inside. They
looked strange, like they had been crying or something.

"Are you two okay?" I asked, staring at their reddened eyes.

Laylen dropped down on the sofa between Aislin and
me and put an arm around each of us. "Yeah, we're fine.
Are you two okay?"

I nodded, giving Laylen a peculiar look. "You're not having problems again, are you?" I whispered, leaning into him. "With your blood thirst, I mean."

He shook his head and squeezed my shoulder. "No, I'm fine, I promise. Alex and I...we just needed to talk about something."

He wasn't telling me something—I could tell, but before I could ask, Alex interrupted.

"Hey, come with me for a moment." He held out his hand to me. "There's something I need to talk to you about."

I looked at Laylen, but he avoided my eyes. So I took Alex's hand and he helped me to my feet.

"You put that thing on?" he asked, noticing the ring on my finger.

I sighed. "I wanted to see if it would do something if I did...it didn't."

He let out a frustrated breath, but didn't say anything. I mean, what would he say? That I needed to be careful and not risk my life like that?

He led me up to my room and shut the door behind us. It was dark, but he didn't flip the light on, nor did he say anything. He just stood there, leaning against the door, and it was driving me crazy because I could feel his gaze on me, sparkling across my skin.

Finally, I clicked the lamp on.

"So, where did you and Laylen go?" I sat down on my bed.

He shrugged, his eyes locked on me. "I just needed to talk to him about something."

"So are you two friends again, then?"

He stepped away from the door and sat down next me. "I guess so." He shrugged. "Well, at least I don't think we'll be beating each other up anytime soon." He let out a loud breath and dragged his fingers through his dark brown messy and in-an-intentional-way hair. "There was just something really important I needed to talk to him about."

"It's not bad, is it?" I asked, picking up a weird vibe from him.

He shook his head, but something in his eyes made my stomach clench. "No, it's not bad." He swept a strand of my hair out of my face and I tensed, remembering how he did the same thing in the vision, right before we died. "It's good…everything will be alright."

My heart skipped a beat, and not in a good way. It skipped a beat in fear, because those were the words he whispered to me in the vision.

"They will?" I asked in a shaky voice. "How do you know?"

He traced the fresh cut on the palm of his hand—the one leftover from our most recent Blood Promise. "I just do."

"Alex," I choked. "What did you say during the Blood Promise?"

He gave me a soft smile. "I'll tell you tomorrow, okay? But right now I just want to lay here with you and think about something else besides the end of the world."

How was I supposed to respond to that? "Okay." Yeah, I guess that worked.

We lay down on my bed, face-to-face, not quite touching, but it was enough for the sparks to flow between us and connect us with an invisible bond.

How could something that felt so good be so wrong?

"I'll leave before it gets too bad," he said, sensing my worry.

I nodded. "Okay."

And then we just lay there, watching one another, letting the silence fade away our worries, until my eyelids grew heavy and I drifted away into a peaceful dream of kisses, warmth, and beautiful green eyes.

Chapter 37

I awoke to an empty room. Alex apparently had kept his word and left when things got bad. I hadn't even felt any weakness, but I guess my sleeping blocked it out. I felt good, actually, for the first time in a while.

I felt charged, like my peaceful dream had re-energized my body.

My stomach let out a growl. Apparently it wanted to be re-energized too.

I got to my feet and padded to my bedroom door. The house was quiet, so I assumed everyone was asleep. As I stepped out into the hall, I noticed something wasn't right. I couldn't quite place my finger on what it was, only that something was off…or missing maybe.

I shook off the feeling and tiptoed downstairs, giving a quick glance into the living room where Alex usually slept. But the couch was empty.

I scratched my head and started to turn away. Maybe he was sleeping in one of the guest rooms, but something caught my eye that made me pause.

An envelope with my name printed on it lay on the table. Something about it made my stomach drop. I flipped on the light and stared at it for a while, too afraid to open it. Finally, with shaking hands I picked it up, tore it open, and took out the folded piece of paper inside it.

I took an unsteady breath and unfolded the paper.

Gemma

I know you may not understand why I need to leave, but I need you to try. I don't believe that your end comes when you think. I believe there is another way, and I'm going to do whatever it takes to find it. But I can't do it while I'm around you. I can't keep hiding what I feel, but if I let it all out, I know it will be the end for both of us. And I can't let that happen.

I will always save you, Gemma, I just need you to hang on until I do.

Alex

The letter slipped from my fingers and floated to the floor like a feather as I stood there, stunned.

I will always save you.

He had said this to me once before, in a dream. But how could he leave without saying anything to anyone? And then it dawned on me, and I took off up the stairs. Without bothering to knock, I barged into the room where Laylen slept and turned on the lights.

He jumped out of bed, startled by my appearance and blinked at me with tired eyes.

"What the heck are you doing?" he asked, rubbing the tiredness from his eyes.

"Please tell me you didn't know," I said, trying to stay as calm as possible.

291

His face fell. He knew.

"But you're supposed to tell me everything," I said in an alarming high-pitch voice. "We tell each other everything."

He sighed and ran his fingers through his blond hair, which was sticking up in all kinds of directions. "I couldn't tell you this."

I walked into the room and sank down on the foot of the bed. "Why not?"

"Because I agreed with him." He sat down next to me. "He needed to leave…it was too hard for him to keep turning off what he felt for you." He wrapped his arm around my shoulder and pulled me against his bare chest. "If he stuck around, you two would end up killing one another."

"But he thinks he can find a way to save me," I whispered. "At least that's what he said in the note."

Laylen pulled me tighter against him. "And maybe he will."

I twisted the ring on my finger—my supposed loophole. My heart was breaking. I got where Alex was coming from. I got that our feelings for one another were getting harder and harder to control. But it didn't make the empty void inside my heart feel any better about him leaving.

He left.

I can't believe he left.

I turned over my hand and stared at the fresh cut. "Do you know what he promised me?" I asked, glancing up at Laylen.

Laylen nodded. "He promised you everything would be alright...and maybe it will."

"Maybe," I said, but the hole in my heart told me otherwise.

We sat quietly, and I could feel the hole in my heart growing bigger with each passing moment.

"He told me to keep an eye on you," Laylen finally said. "While he was gone."

"I don't need to be watched," I said. "I can take care of myself."

"Yeah, you can, but you're also precious cargo," he tried to joke. "And precious cargo needs to be taken care of."

"I am not precious cargo." I frowned more at myself than at him and I could feel this icky bitter feeling building up inside me. "I'm destructive...without me, there would be no star, and therefore, there would be no problems."

He pulled away from me so he could look me in the eye. "That's why he told me to keep an eye on you...he didn't want you to sink into this sad pit of despair because he was gone...You need to keep going. We need to find a way to save you."

"Why does everyone want to save me?" I asked. "And what about Alex? He needs to be saved just as much as I do."

"Everyone wants to save you because you're worth saving, Gemma," Laylen said. "Haven't you figured that out yet?"

I shook my head as tears dripped down my cheeks. I wanted to say something, but there were no words, so instead I leaned my head on his shoulder and cried until I was too tired to keep my eyes open. Then I went back to my bedroom and drifted to sleep, dreaming of fires, stars, and the missing pieces of my heart.

Chapter 38

I woke up to a loud bang that rocked the house. I jumped from my bed, my eyes wildly scanning my surroundings. My room was still filled with the lingering nighttime darkness, and there was a glow from the outside that I assumed was the rising sun.

"What the hell was that?" I mumbled to myself, my heart knocking in my chest. I hurried out into the hall and immediately I realized something was wrong.

The door to my mom's bedroom was open.

It was never open.

My body shook as I made my way to the open door and glanced inside the semi dark room. Then my world crashed to the floor. She was gone. My mom was gone. Nothing remained but the chains, which looked like they had been melted away at the cuffs.

"No..." I shook my head. "No, how did she..."

And then I smelled it. The scent of flowers and freshly fallen rain.

I slowly turned around and was met by a pair of golden eyes.

"You're dead," I stuttered, pinching myself to make sure I was awake.

It stung.

Nicholas raised his eyebrows. "Am I?" He examined his arms over. "Wow! I look really good even for a dead guy."

"N-no." I shook my head, backing into the empty room where my mother should be, but wasn't. "This can't be happening."

Nicholas walked toward me, his hands behind his back. "I think you always kind of knew I wasn't dead...I mean, you have seen me."

"But that was a nightmare," I said in an unsteady voice.

He cocked an eyebrow at me. "Was it?"

"How...I don't..." *Get it together.* "How are you even here? You shouldn't be here."

"Shouldn't I?" For a moment, he looked as confused as I felt, but the look quickly erased. "I mean, I guess technically I shouldn't be here, being dead and all, yet here I am."

"So, you are dead?" I braced a hand on the bed to keep from collapsing to the floor. "How can I still see you then?"

He shrugged, grinning. "Just another amazing thing about you, I guess."

Great. This was the last thing I needed right now. An annoying faerie ghost haunting me. "Okay, so why are you here?"

"Because you changed everything," he said simply, shoving his hands into the pockets of his jeans. "You brought me back."

I gaped at him. "How?"

"By changing the vision."

"But I was supposed to change it...It's what it was supposed to be."

He took another step toward me and I suddenly felt threatened. "Not *that* vision. The other one; the one where I was supposed to take you to Stephan."

My jaw nearly dropped to the floor and I sat down on the bed because my legs would no longer hold me up. "But I..." I was speechless. Never did it occur to me that my father erasing my past would shift future events. Had he known that it would happen?

"So, what?" I asked. "Now I'm stuck with you."

His grin darkened. "Well, you are responsible for my death, aren't you? I mean, if it wasn't for you changing things, I would never have been in that car to begin with."

A guilty knot wove its way into my stomach. "I'm sorry...I didn't know."

"Doesn't matter." He shrugged. "Regardless, you're still stuck with me."

I sank down on the bed, staring at the chains which once held my mom. And now she was gone. Where did she go?

"Don't worry," Nicholas said. "I'm not here to hurt you. I'm here to help you."

"You left the note on my bed, didn't you?" I said. "And you were that annoying talk-show-host voice, weren't you?"

He nodded. "It was the only way I could communicate with you."

"But I can see you now."

"Yes, but you weren't wearing that thing." He pointed to the ring on my finger.

I raised my hand in front of me, staring at the violet gemmed ring enclosed around my finger. "This is why I can suddenly see you?"

He tapped the ring on my finger. "It's the *orbis of silent* or ring of the dead...it gives you the sight of seeing the dead."

"Why would he give this to me?" I stared down at the ring. "How is seeing the dead my loophole?"

He shrugged, sitting down next to me, and I tried not to cringe from his closeness. I mean, the alive Nicholas freaked me out enough, but the dead Nicholas...well, it was beyond creepy.

I had a feeling there was more to his story—that he knew more about the ring then he was letting on. Too bad

Blood Promises didn't last after death because now getting the truth out of him was going to be like pulling teeth.

Nicholas suddenly smirked at the empty chains that once held my mom. "You have such a bumpy road ahead, and you don't even know it."

I pointed at the chains. "Do you know where she went?"

His golden eyes twinkled in the low light of the room. "Perhaps."

I tried to keep my cool. "Can you please tell me?"

He gestured at the window. "The answer is out there."

I stared at the window, not wanting to look, frightened about what I would see.

"Go ahead." He was enjoying this way too much. "Go see the damage you've caused."

I took a deep breath and slowly walked toward the window, my knees knocking together with each step. My palms covered with sweat as I pulled back the curtain.

Garbage cans burned wildly in the streets. A fire lit up the sky. In the next door neighbor's yard, a vampire was feeding off a human, right out in the open, as if it didn't matter, as if all the rules had changed.

I whirled back to Nicholas. "What is this?"

"What did you think was going to happen? That you could change the events of your life and everything would be okay? That you could mess around with visions and everything would be fine?"

My father knew this was going to happen. My father had seen it coming. He tried to show me that there were going to be rough times ahead.

You need to prepare yourself.

"But, why would this happen just from me changing one event of my life?" I asked, motioning at the window were fires blazed vibrantly just outside it. "How could it lead to all this?"

"Don't you remember the butterfly effect?" he asked. "This all happened because I never handed you over to Stephan that day; therefore he had to work harder to try and capture you. So he has been igniting the Mark of Malefiscus on the followers of Malefiscus—something he was going to originally do when the portal opened. He did it so they can help him capture you...And thanks to Stephan and his memory tampering abilities, they think they've been born with the mark." He gestured at the window. "They think this is the way things are supposed to be."

"But this witch, Medea, she said they were waiting for Stephan to perfect the Mark of Immortality before they started hurting people." I glanced at the window, out at the chaos. "Does that mean he's perfected it?"

Nicholas smiled, but didn't answer.

"So can we fix it?" I asked in a panic-stricken voice. "Can we make all the madness out there stop?"

He grinned. "Perhaps..." He glanced at the ring on my finger, and again I assumed he knew more than he was letting on. "But as of now every single creature marked with the Mark of Malefiscus—which is quite a lot thanks to you shifting everything—is roaming the streets." He brushed his finger across the mark on his skin. "My mark is useless, though, since I am dead."

Shaking my head, I sank to the floor, wishing desperately that Alex was here.

"And what if we can't?" I asked, hugging my knees to my chest.

The only answer I got was the fire crackling in the streets.

Jessica Sorensen lives with her husband and three kids in the snowy mountains of Wyoming, where she spends most of her time reading, writing, and hanging out with her family.

Made in the USA
Charleston, SC
24 August 2012